Dream
Of Echoes

Karen C. Webb

ISBN: 0990593819
ISBN-13: 978-0-9905938-1-2

DEDICATION

For my family, Scott, Andrew and Jordan.

Also for my good friend, Leilani, because in the story, a tiny driver evolved into a tiny dancer.

Karen C Webb

Also By Karen C. Webb:

AMERICAN DREAM

RISING STAR

ACKNOWLEDGMENTS

*A special thanks to my true love,
Captain Scotty.
Without his helpful ideas and insight, this story
may have found a permanent home in the
drawer of my desk.*

CHAPTER 1

November 6, 2010

I drove down Interstate Ninety from Seattle, then I cut off onto highway eighty-two and pulled into a gas station. I couldn't get my credit card to work at the pump and I had to take it inside.

"Evening," the clerk said as I handed him my card. He was tall and slim with really blond hair, almost white. Even his eyebrows were a pale blond and his complexion was almost ghostly. "The future is in the past," he said as he swiped my card.

"Excuse me?"

"True love is on the other side," he said as he gave me a big smile and handed me back my card, displaying a row of perfect, even white teeth.

"I'm sorry, I don't understand." I thought maybe this guy was off his meds or something and I turned to leave. I was almost out the door when he spoke again.

"Enjoy your journey," he said.

"Okay, thanks." I waved politely and went on out to pump my gas. What a weirdo, I thought as I stuck the nozzle into the gas tank. I could still see him staring at me out the window beside his cash register. He seemed to be unmoving, just standing stock-still and staring at me.

I quickly forgot the albino weirdo as I continued on my way, my mind drifting back across my mound of problems. I crossed over the Columbia River and into Oregon. The river here was wide and very deep with swift currents and I knew the water had to be barely above freezing. Of course, when wasn't it? It was cold as a witches titty no matter what time of year it was.

I saw a marina on the Oregon side as I crossed the old steel bridge. I quickly took the exit and pulled my car into the marina parking lot. The marina was empty this time of night, but there were lights on the docks that shone across the few pleasure boats moored there, reflecting off the river like huge yellow beacons.

I'd heard on the radio as I drove down that tonight was the time change.

"Don't forget to set your clocks back one hour before you go to bed." The cheery voice of the lady on the radio had been my only company as the miles flew by. "Remember, it's fall back in the fall, spring forward in the spring," she went on.

"Perfect." I had just been forming an idea the last few miles and that old steel bridge looked perfect for it. "I'll do it just as the time changes," I answered the cheery voice on the radio. "And backwards." I nodded my head as I thought about it. I liked the irony. "Fall back in the fall."

I parked my car in the empty lot, put my wallet in the glove box, threw the car keys and my jacket on the seat and started walking. I took my shirt off as I walked toward the bridge and threw it to the side of the road. The cold breeze off the river sent shivers through me, but I kept going, climbing the hill up to the bridge. I was slightly winded by the time I reached it, the wind from the river making it harder to catch my breath. There was very little room between the traffic lanes and the old steel span of the bridge. I stayed close to the steel girders as I walked to the middle. I began climbing slowly up the steel span, which was easier than I'd thought it would be. There were small steel connecting plates running along the outer edge that made it relatively easy to climb.

I was about halfway up when I saw two eighteen wheelers coming down the hill on the Washington side. It's a steep hill and they were picking up speed as they came at me. I flattened myself against the cold steel of the bridge and hoped like hell they didn't see me. I wasn't interested in explaining myself to anyone right now. I'd done enough of that shit lately, thank you very much. The trucks blew by me, side by side, big diesel engines screaming, and the wind from them almost caused me to fall. The old bridge trembled under me as they passed. I tightened my grip and resumed my climb. I pulled myself to the top of the span, sat down and kicked my sneakers off, watching as they hit the swift current below and disappeared.

Would it be high enough? I had never done anything like this before so I really had no frame of reference. I crawled to my knees, then slowly to a standing position atop the steel girder. I stood looking down at the swift current until I felt dizzy. The wind was lifting my hair and it felt like the entire bridge was moving. I stared at the dark, dark river below me for a couple of minutes as I stood there, swaying in the wind. It looked pretty far to the water from this height. I was beginning to think I had screwed up with my hesitation. The longer I stood here, the harder it was to consider letting go and falling—falling on and on, my body tumbling head over heels—then the smack of that water. It would be like slamming into concrete, I was sure of it.

"Shit, I can't do it." I was about to sit down when I heard a man yell from the marina. I looked up and he was outlined under the yellow marina lights, waving at me from the deck of a boat. He yelled something unintelligible, but I could guess what he was thinking. I knew what I'd be thinking if I looked up and saw a guy standing on top of an old steel bridge in the middle of the night.

"Dammit all." I turned with my back to him, and to the river. There was no traffic on the highway in front of me now.

I looked at my watch. It was a nice watch, the last thing Stacey had given me and I didn't want to lose it. It was a white gold with a calendar and a backlight with a dark blue face. It was one minute past two a.m. on November 7, 2010.

I could still hear the man yelling at me. I risked a quick look back and he was running up the hill toward the bridge. I took a deep breath of the cold, wet air, let go of the steel girder and fell backwards toward the cold, dark depths swirling below me.

Earlier that day

I was done with women. Forever. I had never had much luck with them anyway. I had thought I would spend forever with Jocelyn, my high school sweetheart. All I wanted was to settle down with her and start a family. But I guess she had other ideas. She ran off to California with my best friend. She wanted to be an actress, she told me. And she said I was trying to chain her down, that I was holding her back from her dream.

I saw her on TV a couple years ago, walking the red carpet at the Oscars with my best friend beside her, flashbulbs exploding in their faces.

Since then, it's been a string of failed relationships. The latest, Stacey, I proposed to last year. I thought we were happy together. Hell, I *had* been happy, perfectly content in our little love nest in Seattle. Sure, we had our arguments, but what couple doesn't, right?

Then I came home early from work last week and found her in bed with another guy. I wonder how long it had been going on while I was out on the road. It broke my heart; I had really loved her and wanted to spend my life with her.

And maybe things would be different now if the trucking company had given me a route closer to home. Instead, I've been gone so much lately, my girl had to find comfort in the arms of another man. And maybe I wouldn't have been in Phoenix last month if they would've kept me closer to home. I'm sure that minivan swerved in front of me on purpose so they could sue me *and* the trucking company, the bastards. No matter what I did lately, everything just seemed to be falling apart.

I had started with the company right out of high school. Working the docks at their warehouse in Yakima. Eventually, I'd moved up to driver, hauling fruit and vegetables all over the Pacific Northwest. Four years of loyalty I've given that company, then one accident and I'm out on my ass. Well, screw you all.

I jumped in my car and headed east on ninety, then continued east on highway eighty-two, not sure where I was going, but certain a drive would clear my head.

I had sat around the apartment the last two days, my thoughts as dark and gloomy as the thick, gray clouds hanging over Seattle. I had circled several jobs in a newspaper yesterday but I couldn't seem to get motivated to call any of them or leave the apartment. Which I would probably lose now anyway. Stacey had taken care of the bills when I was away and it seems the rent was already two months behind, even before I lost my job. It only served to deepen my depression until finally I had jumped in the car and just started driving.

I had barely even slept the night before, so I probably wasn't thinking too clearly anyway. I had dreamed I was falling. I know, we've all had that dream, right? Well, this time was different. Someone pushed me and I was falling, on and on, falling and falling. I woke up and sat up in bed and, I swear, I was still falling. I had to put a hand on each side of me to stop the fall. In my half-awake state, it felt like I bounced on the bed when I stopped falling, as if I *had* really been falling and had landed on the bed. I know, weird, right?

CHAPTER 2

I suddenly felt strong arms pulling me out of the river. I opened my eyes for a second, but it was pitch black out there, darker than anything I could remember ever seeing. But I thought I saw Indians in the second before I passed out. One on each side of me, a steel grip on each arm dragging me up the bank. I don't mean Indians from India, or even the Native Americans that I've always known. No, Indians with long black braids hanging down a naked chest and buckskin breeches and moccasins. What the hell? It has to be a dream, I told myself. I tried to raise my head, but pain shot through my brain and down my neck and I must have passed out.

When I opened my eyes again, I could see bright sunshine outside, beautiful dappled sunshine between the autumn branches of the trees. I'm still alive, I thought as I stared at the trees. Was I happy about that? I wasn't sure yet; my head felt like it was packed with cotton, or like a massive hangover. But, I was pretty sure I was. I had changed my mind and was about to sit down anyway, right? Then why'd you do it? I asked myself. I don't know, was the only answer I had.

My vision was clearing as I came awake and I could see some kind of white canvas tent over me and I realized I was looking through a hole in the back of it at the river and country surrounding it. And my tent was bouncing up and down. I turned my head, looking at wooden crates and wooden boxes and round wooden kegs on each side of me. What the hell is this? I sat up quickly, too quickly. My head spun and I dropped back down, groaning.

"Whoa," I heard someone call out, and the bouncing subsided. I sat up slowly this time, still trying to get my bearings.

"Perhaps you should lie back, sir. You received quite a nasty bump on your head." The voice was soft and sweet, but yet sounded different than anything I'd ever heard. I followed the sound, turning my head slowly so as not to start it spinning again. I put a hand to my head as I turned it. It felt like some sort of crude bandage was wrapped around my head. Was it a piece of a sheet or rag? I quickly forgot about my head as I looked at the most beautiful girl I'd ever seen, staring at me through a front opening of my tent. Our eyes locked for an instant. I swear she had the prettiest eyes I'd ever seen. They were icy blue with a dark outline circling the blue. There was a shiny, sparkly look to the blue. I wasn't sure if it was excitement or mischief—or maybe her eyes just always sparkled—but they sure were pretty.

"What the hell?" I'm not sure if I said it out loud or only thought it. "Are you guys filming a movie or something?" She was wearing a bonnet like the women wear in western movies. I realized now—my tent was a covered wagon. A bronze skinned young man with shiny black hair braided down his back turned and looked through the opening.

"Strange talk," he said as he grinned at me.

"Yes, Acoose, he does use strange words. Yet I understood some of it."

They got quiet as they stared at me and I could hear the silence. I know it sounds strange, but never in my life have I heard the amount of stillness I heard just then. I could hear the water of the Columbia drifting by beside us. I could hear the breeze rustle the leaves on the trees. A few birds were singing their chirping song. And that was it. The absolute quietness literally hurt my ears, like a buzzing sound running through my brain.

I've driven along the Columbia hundreds of times, running freight out of Seattle and Portland to points east. I've stopped my truck and had lunch sitting on the bank of the river. There's always the sound of traffic, trains, and trucks hauling logs. I thought maybe they had closed interstate eighty-four for filming their movie. God, the traffic tie-up would be a nightmare.

"We are bound for Oregon City. And you, sir? Where were you going when you fell in the river?"

"Oregon City? Why?"

"We are going to the Willamette valley to start a new life. At least that's where most of the immigrants on the Oregon Road are going."

I looked at her, waiting for the punch line, but she only stared back, her blue eyes sparkling. I closed my eyes and rubbed my hands across them, then climbed slowly out of the wagon. My body felt stiff and sore and my head spun crazily as I stepped down. I put my hand up to it again, but the sheet or whatever it was, was in my way. I ripped it off, tossing it back into the wagon, then felt my head again. There was a pretty large lump on the side of my head and I felt a small gash when I touched it. No wonder I was so dizzy. I must have hit my head on something when I jumped in the river, but I certainly didn't remember anything.

There was another young Indian boy outside by the wagon, maybe fifteen years old. He had no shirt on, bronze skin glowing in the sun. He was wearing what appeared to be buckskin breeches and moccasins. Like the other boy, he had shiny black braids of hair hanging over each shoulder. His arms and shoulders appeared strong and wiry. He looked like he'd been spending six hours a day in a gym.

"If you guys are filming a western, it looks like you're being very authentic."

"Strange talk," was his only answer. I shook my head to clear it. But the pretty girl had said immigrants, hadn't she? What freakin' immigrants?

"What the hell is this?" I said as I looked around me. It had to be Hollywood, filming a movie, right? Yet something felt off—strange and different.

When I felt the rocks of the road under my feet, I realized I was barefoot. I looked down. No shirt either. That's right—I remembered now, I'd thrown my shoes and shirt away before I jumped. The only thing I had on was a pair of dark brown trousers. Wait. Rocks on the road? I looked at the road, then looked back the way the wagon had come. Sure as hell, the road was dirt, rocks scattered here and there through it. Not even a regular dirt road either, with marks of plows and ditches alongside. More like a track, with grass growing down the middle of it.

I looked around me, my head aching and my mind swirling. "This is the Columbia River, isn't it?"

The girl had got down from the wagon now and was coming toward me. She had on a pale blue dress that seemed tight at the top and fanned out as it reached to the ground. It made her waist look tiny. She was of a diminutive size, her head barely reaching my shoulder. Not like a hobbit or anything, just a young, skinny girl.

"Yes sir, of course it is." She was looking at me like I was off my rocker. Then where the hell is Interstate Eighty-four? I shook my head some more, but it only made me feel dizzy. There was just the narrow rocky track here, the river on one side and the hills coming down to meet it on the other. It was surreal, it felt familiar, yet strangely foreign.

"My name is Kate Donovan. And this is Acoose and Ojibna. They hired on at Grande Ronde to drive the wagon for me."

"I'm John Baker." I took her small hand and shook it. Her hand was soft, yet felt work-roughened with callouses across the palm. "I guess I'm going to Oregon City too." I really didn't know what else to say. I had to get my bearings first and figure out what the hell was going on. If I was dreaming, hopefully I could wake up soon and end this confusion. I offered my hand to the young boys, but they only stared 'til I dropped my hand. I felt even more confused as I stared at them. What was their problem, anyway?

"You are welcome to share our wagon, Mr. Baker. I lost my husband crossing the Blue Mountains, I think his clothes should fit you."

"I'm sorry to hear that. What happened?"

"He was driving the wagon down an enormous hill and it ran out of control. It rolled over a rather large stone and overturned. He was thrown from the wagon and he died later that night."

"Holy Hell!" I'm not sure if it was sympathy for her or the realization that I had jumped off that bridge and seem to have landed in a wagon on the Oregon Trail! What the hell! How could this be? It felt like it had to be a dream. Yet, it all seemed pretty damn real.

The Indian boy had started the wagon moving again and I walked with Kate beside it, my hand circling repeatedly across the large lump on the side of my head.

Maybe I had a concussion and it was causing hallucinations.

"Could you tell me today's date?"

"November seventh."

"And the year?"

She gave me a strange look. "1847, of course."

"1847?"

"Yes, what year did you think it was?"

I thought maybe I should change the subject before I scared this poor girl. I felt pretty scared myself about then, like nothing was real. Maybe all of it was a dream, and I would wake up soon in my apartment, with Stacey in bed beside me.

"You said you might have some clothes I could borrow? These damn rocks are hurting my feet."

"Of course, Mr. Baker." She turned and, before I could say anything else, she picked up her skirt, stepped up onto the tongue of the moving wagon and pulled herself in.

Jeez, I shook my head and grinned. Tough girl. If she had missed a step, she would have been crushed under the wheel of the wagon. It wasn't the huge wagons I remembered from pictures in school. This one looked more like an old farm wagon, like folks put in their front yard as an ornament or whatever. Except it was a little bigger and wider and the sides of it were built up higher. The white canvas top also looked newer than the rest of it, as if it had been added at a later time. The front wheels were noticeably smaller than the rear, but I'm sure if she would have fell under one, it would have crushed her.

She jumped back out just as quickly with a shirt and a pair of boots in her hand. She met my eyes again as she handed them to me. Her eyes still had a shiny, mischievous sparkle to them and a smile played at the corners of her mouth. I stared at her for a minute; I had a strange urge to kiss her. She had such a beautiful little round face, pale skin and a cute upturned nose with freckles on it. It's a little pixie face, I thought as she stared up at me.

She looked away finally and started walking again, but I caught her looking back at my naked chest a couple of times. I'm pretty broad across the chest and shoulders, just like my old man was.

The wagon had never stopped its slow crawl, so I pulled on the shirt and boots as I walked, hopping on first one foot, then the other as I rammed my feet into them.

CHAPTER 3

Kate walked alongside the wagon, peeking back occasionally when she thought the stranger wasn't looking. She was unaccustomed to seeing a white man without his shirt. She'd never seen her father without a shirt in her life and during her short-lived marriage, her husband had come to her in the dark, fully clothed. This strange young man she'd rescued excited her with his bare chest, his broad, muscled shoulders and arms and his clean-shaven face. Most of the men she knew had long, hairy beards and mustaches, especially on this long journey, where water and time for niceties like a shave were in short supply. Where had this handsome young man come from, that he ended up being pulled from the river and into her wagon? She looked back again as the stranger hopped along, pulling on her husband's boots as he walked. He had put the shirt on but hadn't yet buttoned it and she was intrigued by the bare chest that she could still get a glimpse of. And his disarming smile. It had sent a little thrill through her when he'd smiled at her. It was just a small smile, almost like a knowing smirk, and his eyes had a mischievous light to them. As if he had taken one look at her and instantly read her thoughts. She heaved a sigh as she turned away and continued walking beside the noisy, rattling wagon. He has very expressive eyes, she thought. One of those people who wears their heart on their sleeve, where every emotion is clearly evident in their eyes. And what she'd seen when their eyes had locked, had started a funny feeling in the pit of her stomach.

CHAPTER 4

"You can call me John," I told her as I caught up to her.

"Okay…John." She gave me a beautiful smile, it lit up her ice blue eyes and they sparkled like diamonds.

"How long were you married?" I asked her.

"One month."

"One month?" I was incredulous.

"Yes, my parents both fell sick of the cholera in Wyoming. My mother passed one day and my father the next. My father wished that I should marry Mr. Jacob Donovan who was traveling with our train. He didn't want me left all alone."

"Did you love him?"

"I'm sure I would have come to love him in time." She hung her head, her bonnet hiding her expression. "I'm sorry, I shouldn't have told you that. He was a kind man and a devout Christian." She glanced up at me and I could see the sorrow in her eyes. "Now, I'm not sure what I should do. I don't have relatives in the west. I've been told there will be a party of fur traders going back to the states in the spring."

"Back to the states?" My confused brain was working overtime. History was never my best subject. Then it hit me, Oregon was only a territory in 1847.

"Do you have relatives back east?"

"Only an aging aunt. My father's sister." She shook her head in despair. "I really can't afford the journey back to Ohio and I don't like the thought of burdening my aunt Rose."

"There's got to be something you can do."

Before we could finish the conversation, the wagon master called a halt and the wagons began pulling off the trail and into a clearing. Kate's wagon was the last in line and we had been eating quite a bit of dust as we walked. We followed along as the wagons turned into the clearing between the trees and stopped.

The Indian boys quickly unharnessed the horses and turned them loose. I wanted to be helpful, but I didn't know shit about harnesses. Some of the other men from the wagon train were walking back toward us, including the wagon boss.

"Is this the gentleman you rescued from the river?" He asked Kate as he approached.

"Yes. John Baker, this is our wagon master Isaiah Thomas."

"Pleased to make your acquaintance." The huge, gruff man extended his hand. I felt like my hand disappeared into his big, hairy paw.

"Mrs. Donovan, can we have a word with you?" He jerked his head toward the other men behind him.

"If you'll excuse me, Mr. Baker...I mean John."

"Sure, I guess I can help gather firewood." I had seen women and children scurry about the woods as soon as we stopped, gathering wood for their fires.

The Indian boys already had a fire going when I returned. I dropped the wood I'd brought down near the fire, then took a seat on the ground. My head still hurt a little from whatever I'd hit it on, and I felt a little dizzy. I sat there rubbing the side of my head, the two Indian boys silently staring at me, when Kate returned, looking like she might cry. "They want me to leave the wagon train," she said in despair as she dropped down by the fire, heavy skirts swooshing around her. "Our oxen died along the trail and they said my horses won't be able to pull the wagon across the Barlow road."

I looked over at the two gaunt horses grazing nearby. Both were bays with black stockings and black manes and tails. They were the tall, leggy eastern type, but their ribs and hipbones were showing and I had to agree with the men. They would never make it across a hard trail with that heavy wagon.

"One of the men had a team of oxen that he wanted to trade me, but I can't do that. Nip and Tuck were raised by my father on our farm back in Ohio. My only other option is to float downriver from The Dalles, but it's very expensive and I just don't have the money."

I nodded my understanding, not sure what else I could do.

"They told me I should return to the mission back east of here. It's run by a couple called Whitman. We stopped there for a night on the way here. They were wonderful hosts, but Mrs. Whitman was very busy tending the sick immigrants that had come in. I'm sure they will take us in for the winter. They have a house that immigrants use in winter."

"I'm game," I replied, then at her puzzled look, I said, "sure, sounds good to me, if you don't mind me tagging along."

She nodded her head and those ice-blue eyes met mine. It was like a jolt of electricity; I swear I could see the sparks between us. It was completely unexpected and I sat there dumbfounded, as she began cooking something over the fire. I watched her as she moved deftly about, cooking and readying her meal. She moved lightly, like a deer, and with a grace that surprised me. She almost seemed to float about the camp, her long skirts swishing around her legs. She seemed almost translucent as I stared at her, an amorphous spirit, gliding through the firelight.

She shared her supper with me, bread and the meat she had cooked over the fire, I think it was elk or deer.

She stood up after dinner and took off her bonnet and unpinned her hair. I couldn't take my eyes off her as long blond waves of hair cascaded down her back. It was a golden blonde and had a bit of a curl to it, and it reached almost to her waist. I noticed even the two Indian boys were staring in awe.

"I think I'll turn in, John. You're welcome to sleep under the wagon, in case it rains. I have some extra blankets you can use."

I could only nod like a dazed schoolboy as I followed her to the wagon. She made a pallet for me under the wagon, then she crawled up inside it. I could hear the springs creak as she moved about over me. I lay on my back and stared at the bottom of the wagon as I thought about the tiny, beautiful girl sleeping just above me. It seemed like this young girl had endured some pretty rough times in her life, and I felt inexorably drawn to her. I felt a strange male need to help and protect her. And, as I lay there, I wondered how it was I had come to be here. Was it a magic bridge? Or did it have something to do with the time change? I had no idea, and I felt a mixture of excitement at such an unbelievable adventure, but also a fear that I could be stuck here.

I dreamed of Kate that night as I slept under her wagon. We were standing on a steel bridge overlooking a river. It was a little fuzzy in the dream, but I think it was the Columbia River. It wasn't the same bridge I had jumped from, but it was similar. The Pacific Northwest has a lot of old steel bridges; it could have been anywhere. I could see Kate's long blond hair blowing in the wind and I could feel the wind against my face. I took her hand in my dream, and together, we jumped off the bridge. I could see her skirts floating around her as we fell and, just before we hit the water…I jerked awake and sat up so quick, I cracked my head on the bottom of the wagon. I was disoriented and it took a moment to remember where I was. The fire had died and the darkness was absolute. Clouds had rolled in; I could just see the moon peeking through. But the stars were completely hidden, blocking any light they might have provided. I rubbed the new lump I'd given myself on the underside of the wagon, then held my hand in front of my face. I could barely make it out, even though it was only about six inches from my eyes. I went camping with my dad and brothers as a kid and I had thought the darkness underneath the huge trees in Washington was pitch black. But I don't think I'd ever seen anything to compare to this darkness. Not even a distant city to brighten the horizon.

I finally drifted back into a restless sleep, with a huge rock poking me in the back the rest of the night.

We watched the wagon train roll out the next morning at dawn, then the Indian boys hitched up the team and we started slowly moving east. When Kate explained her plan to the boys, they refused to go, both of them shaking their heads.

"No, we no go," Acoose said.

"Bad medicine," the other one chimed in, also shaking his head.

Kate looked near tears again as we walked so I put my arm around her shoulders and squeezed. "It'll be okay," I told her. "I'll go with you." Truthfully, I didn't know what else I could do. I didn't know if I was stuck in this time, but it was better to tag along and give her a hand, than wander this wilderness alone. And she seemed like she could use a hand as well.

Kate leaned her head into my shoulder and I felt some better. How could this cute young girl stuck out here on a dusty wagon trail smell so good? She smelled like my blankets back home, after being freshly laundered and hanging out on the line all day. Yep, that's it. Like the fresh autumn air. I left my arm across her shoulders as we walked beside the slow moving wagon, her small body bumping occasionally against my side. I think it was probably a little forward of me, but she didn't seem to mind.

"Why don't the boys want to come with us," I asked her. So far, they were still driving the wagon, but I could see them up on the seat, heads close together, whispering.

"I don't know," she sounded so sad, I squeezed her shoulder a little tighter. "They won't say anything other than 'bad medicine.' I have no idea what they mean by that, but you know, their beliefs are quite different than ours."

"Yeah, I know. Well, I hope you don't mind me tagging along?" She looked up at me and smiled. "I would be very grateful for your company, John Baker."
I studied the countryside as we walked. I had traveled this same area hundreds of times in my truck, but I couldn't recognize anything. Even the river itself looked different. Without the dams holding it back, it rolled along at a shallower, steadier pace than I had ever seen it. Usually there were tugboats pushing barges down the middle and freight trains and traffic running alongside. And I seemed to remember more trees along it than what I was seeing now. It was absolutely pristine without all the human intervention that I was used to. A primordial wilderness untouched by man. Not just the river, the whole area was filled with primeval forests and empty

hills, with no human influence other than the rocky trail we strode. No houses or towns, no power lines or cell phone towers. I looked across the river to the Washington side. Normally I could see houses and roads zigzagging up the steep, brown hills. Now, I could only see a small group of fat Indian ponies grazing across the hills. There were a few cranes and other water birds standing along the edge of the river, dipping their beaks under occasionally, fishing I assumed. I had never given it much thought before, what this land looked like before white people moved in and brought their *progress,* but looking at it now, I decided I liked it much better this way.

CHAPTER 5

We must've made twelve or more miles that day. My feet and legs felt like it was a hundred miles. And wearing someone else's boots didn't help. I couldn't remember the last time I was this tired. I noticed one of the horses taking stumbling steps, too. I bet his feet hurt as much as mine right now. Kate seemed tireless and those Indian boys, I bet they could've ran a marathon right now, and won it, too.

We camped that night on a hill overlooking the river and a small Indian village along the banks. I could see the light of their fires beside the river. I wasn't sure, but I thought we were near the place where I had jumped from the bridge. I wondered if I jumped back in, if I would be instantly transported back home. Of course, that old steel bridge wasn't here, but maybe that wouldn't matter. Then I looked at Kate as she sat by the fire. Her face had an orange glow from the flames and the flickering light made her eyes dance. I leaned back on my hands, away from the light of the fire and looked up at the stars. The sky was literally lit up with stars.

Millions upon millions of twinkling lights that seemed to brighten the night. The sky behind the stars had a blackness to it that I'd never seen before. Maybe because there were no cities here or even headlights of a vehicle to brighten the night. The stars stood out against the blackness with a twinkling brilliance unlike any night sky I had ever seen. The absolute quiet and beauty of a place I'd known all my life and never much cared for, made me wonder if I really *wanted* to go back home.

Not to mention the beautiful young girl across the fire from me. I bet she'd never been in a single's bar in her life. I was tired of the party girls who had no direction in their lives. It figures, I'd had to travel back through time to meet the kind of girl I'd always been looking for.

We woke at the crack of dawn, I in my bed under the wagon, Kate from her place inside it. It was getting damn chilly at night, but the heavy woolen blanket she'd given me really seemed to hold the body heat in.

She started the fire while I gathered firewood before we realized those two Indian boys were gone. They had crept away in the night like a couple of, well…Indians, I guess. I saw Kate's eyes getting misty when she realized it, but then she turned her back for a bit, getting coffee and breakfast going on the fire.

I was helping her hitch up the team, when all of a sudden the horse I was holding—Tuck—I think, reared straight up in the air, letting out a squeal that curled the hair on the back of my neck. He yanked the reins from my hands and took off like a shot. Kate grabbed her horse's rein and led him in circles, trying to quiet him.

Then a big mountain lion came over the hill about a hundred yards away from us, his eyes intent on the horse that had ran away. Kate handed me the reins and ran to the wagon, emerging with a rifle. It was an old musket variety and it looked too big for her to handle. The barrel was so long it looked like she could hardly hold it. I looked toward the river where the panicked horse was running straight toward it, with the mountain lion closing the distance. It seemed too far for a shot, but I heard her rifle boom and the other horse almost ripped the reins from my hand. Sure enough, the kick from that big, long rifle set her right down on her ass. As the report of the rifle echoed off the river and surrounding hills, I saw first the mountain lion fall, then the horse went head over hills, stirring up dust as the huge body landed, half in and half out of the water. Had her bullet went through the mountain lion and into the horse?

CHAPTER 6

Kate had scrambled to her feet and was running down the hill toward the river, damn near as fast as the horse had, her skirts swishing around her legs until I thought they would trip her. A couple of Indian men from the village had already run over; they were kneeling over the horse and shaking their heads. The horse lifted his head to look at them, but didn't try to rise. Kate reached the horse and dropped to her knees, flinging the rifle to the ground as I slowly made my way down the hill, leading the other horse slowly along with me.

Before I could reach her, I saw her lift the rifle, aim it at the horse's head and pull the trigger. I stopped, the horse yanking back, almost ripping the reins from my hand again. I reached Kate finally and saw her put her head down on the horse's neck as she cried.

The two Indian men had turned away from her and went discreetly back to their village. I squatted on the ground beside her and put my arm haltingly around her.

She turned and put her head into my chest and I wrapped both arms around her and held her as she cried.

I knew what it was like to lose an animal you loved. My dog Skip was around for most of my childhood. Losing him had been like losing a family member and a best friend at the same time.

"His leg was broken, I had to do it," she said between sobs.

"I know," I whispered into her hair. I rested my chin on top of her head as I held her.

Before long, the Indians returned with help. There were about six men altogether from their village. I jumped in too as the men grabbed the horse's forelegs and drug it from the water. We thanked them for their help, then with a final look at her friend Tuck, Kate started slowly back up the hill.

Now we had a heavy wagon and only one horse. We stood there staring at it, neither of us speaking. "Maybe we can trade with the Indian's for a horse," I finally suggested.

"Sure, except the only thing I have left worth trading would be the wagon itself." She stared at the wagon, lost in thought. "I think my father left a packsaddle in there." She climbed into the wagon and I heard her rummaging around, mumbling to herself.

She emerged a few minutes later with an old wooden packsaddle. I held the horse while she strapped it on, then she went back into the wagon and started tossing things out.

"Food and clothes, that's all we will be able to carry," she said as she climbed out and stood amidst the bundles she'd thrown out. "Not that there's much more in there, we left my mother's bureau by the trail in Kansas because the wagon was too heavy to ford a river. Then her trunk was smashed when the wagon overturned with my late husband. All I really have left is my mother's jewelry box."

"Bring it," I told her. "If I have to carry it in my hand, I'll take it for you."

"Oh, thank you so much, Mr... I mean, John." She blushed as our eyes met, then she quickly turned away and climbed back into the wagon. She climbed back out with a bundle of rawhide strips in her hand.

"What're those for?"

"We can use them for tying our bedrolls on the packsaddles. I don't have any rope so...you never know, they may come in handy."

We packed the food into the panniers that hung from the packsaddle. I helped her roll the clothes and her jewelry box into our sleeping blankets and we tied them onto the saddle with the rawhide strips and started on our way, leading the horse behind us.

We led Nip back down to the Indian village and asked around until we found a man who spoke some English. Kate offered him a trade of the wagon and he translated to the other men standing around him. The men went through their village and came back with an assortment of trade goods. One man brought a haunch of venison, one brought needles and thread and a small pouch of black powder for Kate's rifle and another had what I thought was potatoes, but Kate said was Camas bulbs.

The Indian man nodded and smiled at me. "Camas," he said, "roast in coals."

"Okay." I nodded my thanks to him.

We gathered up the goods and added them to the packsaddle while the men went up the hill. Those Indian men grabbed the tongue of the wagon and pulled it down to the village themselves. Damn, but these people were tough!

We only made a few miles that day. The horse, Nip, had sore feet. His front hooves were worn down to the quick from the almost two thousand mile journey he'd made.

"He needs shoes," I told Kate. "At least on the front."

"I know," she hung her head as if ashamed. "They were never supposed to pull that wagon," she said angrily. "If my father had any idea what this journey is like, I'm sure he would never have made the decision to come."

"I'm sorry you've lost so much." I said awkwardly. I put my hand on her arm as I said it and she brought her hand up into mine. We continued on silently for a bit, her small hand warm in mine.

When we stopped to make camp, I realized Nip wasn't the only one with sore feet. Not only was I more used to driving the miles every day than walking them, but the slightly large boots had worn blisters on both my heels. I sucked in a breath as I pulled each one off. The blisters felt like someone was holding a lit match on them. Kate brought some sort of salve from one of her packs and applied to both my feet. I leaned back on my elbows and relaxed as she worked on them. Her touch was so gentle and tender, I think I drifted off to sleep.

I woke up shivering a while later, the cold, damp ground had seeped through my whole body. It had grown dark while I dozed and I saw Kate sitting by the fire, stirring a pot bubbling over it. "Oh, you're awake. Come and have some soup."

I crawled slowly to my feet, every muscle stiff and complaining. I was used to sitting behind the wheel of a truck all day, not walking for hours and chasing after runaway horses. I saw she had wrapped pieces of cloth around my sore feet.

"Thank you for that," I told her, pointing at my feet.

"You're very welcome, John Baker."

I slipped my feet gingerly back into the over-large boots, keeping the cloth in place. I tried a few steps, slowly at first, then quicker as I realized the pain was almost gone.

"You worked miracles," I told her happily as I sat down beside her.

She giggled. "Not miracles really, but I'm happy it helps."

She hadn't brought much for dishes so we shared the soup straight from the pot. She had broken up pieces of jerky, potatoes and onions into her soup and she brought out a couple of cold, hard biscuits. I was starving and the food tasted wonderful.

She said they had traded the Indians at Grande Ronde for peas, onions and potatoes. "Although there's not much left now," she finished.

"Well, it's delicious," I answered.

She had also roasted some of the Camas bulbs and they were wonderful and steaming hot when she pulled them from the coals. They tasted much like a baked sweet potato, only a little stringier.

"If we had anything worth trading for, we could have got some more horses at Grande Ronde. Their Cayuse ponies were some of the fattest, prettiest horses I've ever seen."

"It would have been helpful," I answered. "Were there a lot of Indians there?"

"Oh, yes. The Indian women were trading their beadwork with the women, while the men traded horses and oxen and supplies."

I thought about all the signs I had read along the highway over the years, depicting the journey these folks had made. It was unbelievable to be looking at it firsthand now. Well...more than looking at it. I guess I was living it too.

When I finished eating, I leaned back against a log with my cup of coffee. The hot soup was bringing some life back to my tired body.

"Where are you from, John?"

I looked up at her and when our eyes met, she blushed and lowered her gaze.

"I'm sorry, I hope I'm not being too forward. I was only curious."

"No, not at all. I grew up in the Yakima Valley and now I live in Seattle."

"What do you do there? For a living, I mean."

"I drive a truck." Shit! It had slipped out before I realized it. I must be tired.

"You drive a what? A team?"

My mind was racing. Do I tell her the truth or make something up? I stared at her across the fire for a long minute, and then just started talking. "I'm from the year 2010. I jumped off a bridge the other night when the autumn time change started and I landed here."

I watched her face go from shock to horror to disbelief. "I don't believe you." She was starting to look angry now.

"I swear it's the truth. I was mad and hurt and confused and I jumped in my car and drove until I saw that bridge. Then I jumped. Or let go and fell backwards, to be exact."

"What did you say? A caa...r?" She stretched the word out, as if she needed to get a feel for it. Her face had softened, but only a little. "Is this why you speak a little strangely at times and say words I don't understand?"

"Yeah, I'm sure it is," I laughed softly as I saw comprehension sinking into her face. I fished around in my pants pocket and found the change I still had there. "There you go." I held up a shiny quarter. It was one of the new ones with the name of a state on the back.

She held it up by the light of the fire, turning it this way and that until she had read every bit of it. "It says 2009," her voice was now filled with wonder, she sounded young, almost childlike with awe. When she'd finished perusing it, she looked back over at me. "I can't believe this is really happening. We must not tell anyone of this. Most people are afraid of what they don't understand."

"Are you afraid?" She stared at me and our gazes locked, her blue eyes had an amused and excited sparkle, but I didn't see fear.

"No. You won't hurt me, John Baker. I can see it in your eyes. The kind of man you are. Or at least the kind of man you would like to be."

As I stared into her eyes, I was pretty sure this was one of the defining moments of my life. Jumping off a bridge and falling back through time hadn't affected me the way this woman had. Was I falling for her?

CHAPTER 7

We added an extra log on the fire and made our beds beside it. The temperature had dipped and I told her it was probably snowing up in the Cascades. We didn't have the wagon for shelter now; if it rained or snowed, we would be exposed to the elements. I pulled the heavy blanket over me and immediately drifted off.

I woke up shivering sometime late in the night; the fire had gone out, the moon had set and it was pitch black out there. I jumped and damned near peed my pants when I felt the blanket lift and a warm body slide in next to mine. Then I heard Kate giggle.

"I'm sorry, John, but I'm freezing." She was shivering uncontrollably.

I sat up and pulled her blankets over us too, then lay back down on my side and wrapped my arms around her, pulling her against my chest. I rested my chin on top of her head and slept contentedly until the sun woke us, shining in our eyes.

"Close the blinds and come back to bed," I said sleepily before I realized where I was.

Kate giggled and sat up, throwing the covers off me. "Are you really from the future?" She still had the quarter in her hand, she must have slept with the damn thing. Now she was holding it up in the early morning light, studying it closely.

"No, I'm from the present and I traveled back to the past," I joked. "That means *you* are from the past."

She looked at me, her blue eyes dancing happily. "Now you're in my present, which means you're from the future. It's like a riddle."

I chuckled at her as I started the fire and made coffee.

"How did you get here?" she asked, holding the steaming coffee cup I had given her near her face.

"I really don't know. Like I said, I jumped off the bridge and woke up here."

She stared at me with a serious look to her blue eyes, as if she was still trying to figure out if I was being honest.

"I swear it's the truth," I told her. "I'm as confused by it as you."

"Then it's not something that happens a lot in your time?"

"No. As far as I know, time travel has always been proven to be impossible."

We chewed on some cold jerky with our coffee, then loaded up her sore-footed horse. He was some better, but still moving gingerly on his front feet, taking small, painful steps.

"I have an idea, do you have more of the cloth you used on my feet?"

"Yes, there's an old sheet." She pulled it from her blankets and handed it over. I tore strips and wrapped Nip's front hooves, tying the sheet in a small knot just above the hoof. The horse took a few awkward steps, lifting each foot high until he got used to his bandages.

The stones in the trail were easier for him to negotiate and soon he was walking at a more normal pace.

"What gave you that idea? I never would have thought of putting cloth on a horse's feet." Kate asked curiously.

"Saw it on a TV show," I answered without thinking.

"What's a TV show?"

"How can I describe it? Um… a TV is a box with moving pictures in it."

She was staring at me, unbelieving.

"Of course, you gave me the idea also."

Kate's brow wrinkled as she looked at me.

"My feet feel so much better with the cloth you wrapped them in."

"Aah…" She seemed placated.

"We also have machines that have replaced the horse for transportation," I told her.

"Really? Are they any faster?" She still seemed to be having trouble believing me.

"How many miles a day did you make coming across this trail from Missouri?"

"Usually between ten and twenty."

"Well, I usually make five or six *hundred* miles a day in my big truck."

"Now I'm sure you're fooling me, John Baker. Why, we could have been here in just days, instead of six months."

"No fooling, it's all true. We also have planes that fly through the air and we've sent men to the moon."

"Why would you do that? Are they still there?" Her face had taken on the childlike wonderment again as she tried to imagine it.

"No, they're not still there," I chuckled. "We did it to prove we could and to bring stuff back for scientists to study."

We walked in silence for a bit as she digested the information. Then she asked me, "What will you do now? Are you going to return to *your* time?"

"I don't even know if I can. I've been thinking about it and it seems to me, if the time change was the reason for this, then I would have to wait until the spring, when the clock moves forward."

"What is a time change? I've never heard of someone changing time."

I had a good laugh at that. "I guess you don't practice the time change, then?"

She only looked more confused so I did my best to explain it.

"I never cared much for it myself," I told her. "It's called 'Daylight Savings Time.' We move our clocks back one hour in the fall, and ahead an hour in the spring. Fall back in the fall and spring forward in the spring."

"What on earth for?"

"Hell, I don't know. It's supposed to save daylight, but I never saw the point."

"If you go back to your time in the spring, can you take me with you? I want to see the future and these machines you speak of."

"I don't know Kate, if it didn't work, we'd probably both be leaping to our deaths."

"I'll take the chance. I've always felt like destiny had something more in store for me than being a wife and mother. I want to fly like a bird," she yelled, then she ran down the trail ahead of me, flapping her arms and laughing.

Her high spirits improved my own mood and I temporarily forgot about my sore feet, my aching muscles, and the fact that I may never again see my dear, sweet mother and my two rowdy brothers.

When she had settled down and had once again matched the slow pace of her sore-footed friends, it was my turn to question her.

"Tell me about your journey," I said as I draped my arm over her shoulder.

Her face hardened as she thought about the arduous trip. "When we started out, we had plenty of everything. My father even bought a milk cow in Kansas. We had fresh milk every day until we lost her crossing a river. She didn't make it through the strong current and was swept away downriver. We did fine traveling along the Platte River, plenty of food for our wagon train and good grazing for our stock. But after fording the South Platte, firewood became scarce and we resorted to using buffalo chips for our fires. We found a rocking chair someone left behind and I saw my first prairie dog town." She hesitated as we watched a flock of geese overhead, flying south for the winter. "We were near Chimney Rock when we saw our first buffalo. It was really indescribable. First we heard a roar in the distance and we could see a cloud of dust. Then the herd crossed in front of us." She took a deep breath and sighed as she remembered. "We could see for miles, and as far as the eye could see, the herd went on and on. It brought our wagon train to a halt and we probably sat near to an hour as they crossed. Some of the men on horseback went after them and they killed several. The meat was actually very tasty."

Now I sighed. I didn't want to tell her how those huge herds were eventually almost wiped out.

"Go on," I told her.

"After that, we reached Wyoming territory. We camped for a night by Rock Independence, but it was already mid-July. We should have made it there around Independence Day. There were names and dates of travelers carved into it. My father carved Donovan into it and underneath our name, he carved July, 1847."

"That's cool. I've heard of Independence rock, but I've never had a chance to see it."

"It's still there?"

"You bet it is. Names and dates, all of it. It's a historical marker and people go to visit it. The Oregon Trail is marked along the way as well. There are still wagon ruts in the West, carved into the rock from so many wagons. In the future, we haven't forgotten the strong people like yourself who settled the west."

"I haven't done anything," she said in a small voice, staring at the ground as she walked.

"Anyway, go on with your story," I prodded.

"We came through South Pass and forded so many creeks and rivers, I lost count. We saw several graves alongside the road and near a stream, we came upon a man's skeleton. There was a hole in the skull. I think the poor man had been robbed and murdered. We camped for a night at Green River. We lost two from our wagon train there. They called it 'mountain fever.' It was really a frightful trip. The heat and the dust were unbearable. We were losing our oxen to Alkali water. There was very little grazing and there was dead livestock along the road. Then my folks took sick." She stopped and heaved a sigh.

"It's okay, I know the rest of the story." I put my arm back around her as we walked along, offering what comfort I could.

"No," she said, shrugging my arm away and turning to stare up at me. "You don't. I wasn't even able to give my parents a decent burial. We buried each of them in an unmarked grave in the middle of the road... Due to the Indians in the area," she explained at my confused look. "They dig them up to take whatever belongings they have. So we buried them in the road, and then drove the wagons across the graves to conceal them."

"Good God," I said softly. Some of the shit these people had dealt with was just unimaginable.

"But then we came to the soda springs," her voice brightened as she remembered. "There was hot water shooting up out of the rock, and yet the spring had cold, bubbly soda water. I drank so much, I got a stomachache."

I laughed at her. "It's funny, the things we take for granted in my time, but you're so thankful for in your time."

We grew quiet for a bit, each lost in our own thoughts as we walked along the rough road. I began humming a tune as I walked.

"What's that?" She asked.

"Oh, just a song." I hummed a few more bars, then sang some of it for her. It was an oldie that my mother used to sing as she worked around the house.

"That's beautiful. Sing some more."

I finished the song, or at least as much as I could remember. Then I handed her the horse's rein as a thought struck me. I moved ahead of her down the trail and started singing rock songs. I sang and danced around like an idiot while she laughed at me. I did the robot dance and even moonwalked down the trail.

She laughed until tears streamed from her eyes. "I like your future songs," she laughed merrily. "What's that dance you did? When you went backwards?"

"It's called the 'moonwalk'," I told her. She handed over the reins and tried it herself, lifting her skirts and sliding her feet awkwardly backwards.

"That's it, you're getting it." I watched her in amazement. She had so much spirit and vitality— moxie—my dad called it. She made me forget about my aching muscles and sore feet. "Our worlds are so far apart," I told her when she settled down and went back to walking alongside me. "I may as well be from another planet."

"Maybe I would fit into your world better," she said and she took my arm as we walked, her small hand tucked just above my elbow.

"I don't know about that, it would probably be a little scary for you."

"I wouldn't be scared," she said emphatically. "I love adventure."

I let the subject drop for now and pointed down the road. "There's a wagon up there."

CHAPTER 8

There was a wagon in the middle of the road with two mules hitched to it and a grizzled old man sitting beside it. He stood up when he heard us coming. "Hello." He offered his hand and I shook it. "I'm Jeremiah Harding."

"I'm John Baker and this is Kate Donovan."

"I'm sorry if my wagon is blocking the road, the wheel came off the axle. I sure could use a hand fixing it."

"Sure." I handed the reins to Kate and circled around the wagon to give him a hand.

"Alright, John. I'm going to lift it and you slide the wheel back on."

"Okay." I was a little skeptical. The wagon was piled high and covered with a piece of canvas. It looked like we needed a hi-rise jack for it. Jeremiah crawled under the wagon and put his back against the underside of it. I took the wheel and rolled it over near the axle when I saw what he was going to do. He began slowly standing, using his whole body to lift the wagon. I didn't

41

believe what I was seeing, but the wagon was slowing rising. He was almost to a standing position, hunched over with the weight of the wagon on his back. I pushed the wheel onto the axle quickly.

"Got it," I called out. He dropped to his knees and let his breath out in a whoosh. He'd been holding his breath I guess, as he held up the weight of the wagon. It had to weigh as much as a small car.

When we had the wheel repaired, Jeremiah sat down in front of his small fire, wiping the sweat from his brow with the back of his hand. He coughed a couple times, a deep, hacking cough that seemed to rattle his chest.

"Can I offer you kind folks a meal?" he asked.

"Sure," I answered quickly. I didn't know about Kate, but I was starving. I was beginning to lose weight on this adventure, eating and working the way these people did. Jeremiah went back to his wagon, lifted the canvas cover, and began pulling out items for cooking.

I helped Kate gather more firewood and we gathered around the fire for coffee and venison. Jeremiah even had potatoes he'd gotten from the Indians to go with it. That deer meat tasted better than the finest restaurant in Seattle.

Kate laughed at me as I ate ravenously. "It's good to see a man with a healthy appetite," she said with a gleam in her eyes. "We had so much sickness coming west, no one was eating very well."

"Where are you two headed?" Jeremiah asked. He was looking at me, but Kate answered before I could.

"Waiilatpu," she told him. "We were going to the Willamette Valley until we lost all our stock. Now we're just looking for a place to overwinter."

Jeremiah gave me an odd look. He probably wasn't used to having a woman speak up for a man, but since I didn't know what a Waiilatpu was, I figured I better keep my mouth shut.

"It is getting pretty late in the season to make the Barlow road," he answered pensively.

"Yes, our wagon train laid by too many days with sickness, we fell further and further behind."

"Well," Jeremiah said slowly, "I hear there's been a lot of sickness at the Whitman Station too."

Kate nodded. She too, had heard about pioneers coming into the station with illness.

"I tell you what," Jeremiah drawled, scratching his long beard, "I have a cabin up on the Walla Walla, you folks are welcome to stop in there. It's not much, but it has everything you should need to get you through the winter."

Kate was shaking her head emphatically. "Thank you, Mr. Harding, but we really couldn't impose. I'm told that the Whitman's have a house built for the immigrants and perhaps we can be of use to them."

"It's no imposition, young lady. I'm meeting a party from the Hudson's Bay Company east of here to unload these furs, then I'm working my way south and east for the winter. I won't be back through here til spring."

"Thank you, Jeremiah." I shook his hand. "We just might take you up on it."

We helped Jeremiah clean and put away his cooking utensils, then we shook hands and parted company. We were turning northeast to follow the Walla Walla River, while he headed on east along the Oregon Road.

"What's Waiilatpu?" I asked her when we were walking again.

"It's the Indian word for the mission. It means, 'where the rye grass grows,' I think."

"Oh, alright." I tried it out, rolling the word off my tongue. "Waiilatpu."

We made another fifteen miles or so that day, fueled by Jeremiah's delicious venison. We made camp in a sandy clearing beside the Walla Walla River. Kate brought out a piece of a net and showed me how to catch fish with it. We dined well that night on trout fried over the fire, with a couple of Camas bulbs to go with it.

I sat back in the sand afterward, pulled off my boots and stuck my toes in the cool, white sand. It felt so good to my aching feet, I leaned back on my elbows as I dug them in deeper. Kate giggled as she watched me.

"I want to try that, too." She sat down and pulled off her own boots and buried her feet in the sand.

"Oh, it does feel nice," she giggled some more. "My mother would be appalled."

"Why?" I asked her as I leaned back on the packsaddle, digging my feet even deeper into the sand. I watched her as she sat in the sand, her long blond hair blowing in the breeze, her bare feet stuck in the sand. She's even prettier loosened up, I thought. Her blond hair was so heavy and thick, it made her small pixie face look even smaller.

"No bonnet, no shoes, my hair loose. 'You look like an Indian maiden,' that's what she would tell me."

"That's not such a bad thing. Some of the prettiest women I've ever seen are Native American. There was a Navajo girl down in Arizona one time. She was waitressing at a café I stopped into. She had to be about six feet tall with a slim, perfect figure and long, long legs like a model. And she had that really shiny black hair, damn near down to her waist. Beautiful girl."

"Really, you don't mind if my skin turns brown from the sun?" She had moved as she talked and was now sitting beside me, her head on my shoulder and her toes back in the sand.

"Honey, where I come from, girls pay a lot of money to tan their skin." I put my hand under her chin and turned her face up to look at it. The sun had only put a little color into her small, pale face and added a few more freckles across her nose. I leaned down and kissed her before I realized what I was doing. At first soft and gently, then, as she responded in kind, I kissed her deep and passionately. I broke the kiss finally, pulling away before I lost all control. Both of us were out of breath and I could see her eyes blazing with heat.

"I've never been kissed like that before, John Baker. Is that how it's done in your world?"

"Honestly, little one, that was a new one for me, too. I've been around the block a time or two, but you took my breath away." And with that, I grabbed her and kissed her again, long and deep. I couldn't get enough of the smell and taste of her. She still had the smell of fresh laundry and autumn air about her. I don't know how she did it. I figured I had to be getting pretty gamy. I had changed into the only other set of her husband's clothes she had brought for me and we had both bathed in the icy waters of the Columbia, but it was definitely not the hot shower and shampoo I was used to. She had even showed me how to make my own toothbrush from the branches of willow trees, but a part of me craved the comforts of home. I pulled away again from the passion of her kiss and stared into her shiny, ice-blue eyes.

"I want to stay with you, John Baker," she whispered as she stared back. "Here, or two thousand and ten, I don't care which century. My heart feels that we belong together. Providence brought you across time for me."

Was it true? Was this my destiny? As I looked deep into those beautiful blue eyes, I thought maybe it *was* true. I stood up slowly, lifted her up out of her place in the sand and carried her to my bed.

CHAPTER 9

I felt like a new man as we strolled along the next morning. I whistled as I walked and Kate tried her best to imitate my whistle. I laughed and put my arm around her as we walked. Try as she might, she couldn't seem to form her lips into a whistle.

"It's because your lips are made for kissing," I told her as I pulled her closer and kissed her mouth hard. She wouldn't be deterred, and she practiced all morning as we walked along, until by our noon break, or nooning, as these folks called it, she was whistling a perfect imitation of my tune.

We were sitting by the fire, having coffee, when I heard a stick break in the brush behind us. The horse's head came up from his grazing, he pricked his ears toward the sound and snorted. Now, I'm no woodsman, but the little hairs on the back of my neck stood up. I jumped up and backed away from the fire just as a white man in dirty brown clothes came out of the brush toward me. He was skinny and greasy and grizzled and I don't think he'd seen a bathtub for quite some time.

Kate had stood up too and she moved toward her horse, where her rifle was still tied on the packsaddle.

"I didn't mean to scare you folks." The man held his empty hands out toward us.

Regardless of his words, I sensed a malevolence as I backed slowly away. I jumped, my heart pounding, when I heard another stick break in the brush behind me. I had backed all the way to it and as I whirled around, I could just see the muzzle of a rifle coming through the brush. I didn't even think, I just reacted. I kicked the muzzle up, and then dove through the brush, landing on top of the man holding it. He was dirty too and he smelled horrible. I punched him once on the jaw, but he was quick. He was on his feet before I had a chance to move in on him. The rifle had fallen on the ground between us. I kicked it behind me, then jumped on the guy, pushing him back into the undergrowth. I heard Kate scream behind me, but my hands were pretty full at the moment. As the guy went down into the bushes, I went down on top of him, one knee in his groin, the other hand on his throat.

"We're gonna kill you and take your horse and your woman," he growled from underneath my hand that was still squeezing his throat. I saw his eyes bulge as I squeezed harder and harder on his throat. His hands came up, but I was too damned mad to be stopped. I swatted his hands away like a pesky fly and squeezed ever harder. I held on to his throat until his bulging eyes closed and he stopped flailing, I didn't know if he'd passed out or I had killed him and at the moment, I didn't care.

I ran back through the bushes to help Kate, grabbing the man's rifle as I went. Before I made it through the undergrowth, the man called out to me.

"Come on out," he yelled to me. "We just want your horse. And maybe I'll have my way with this pretty little thing here." He smiled an evil smile, his teeth brown and crooked. They were standing across the fire from me, facing me. The greasy guy was behind her, one arm around her waist, the other holding a knife to her throat. It was a huge, shiny knife with a thick blade curving down to a sharp point. Like the old-time Bowie knives, I thought. My heart was pounding so loud, I swear I could hear it.

"Put the gun on the ground," he yelled at me. I looked into Kate's eyes, they were wide with terror and desperation. I bent slowly, setting the rifle gently on the ground in front of me, never taking my eyes off the two of them.

"Now, lead that horse over here," the greaseball commanded. I moved slowly left, toward the horse, watching Kate's eyes. The man's eyes followed me and, as I watched Kate, I saw her move quickly, thrusting her elbow back into the man's gut, and then, as his arm came up, she stooped out from under the knife. She grabbed the coffee pot from the fire and hurled it backward toward the man.

I was already running as the scene was playing out in front of me. I was leaping across the fire as the coffee pot was bouncing off the guy's head, spilling boiling hot coffee across his forehead and face. He let out a howl and took a step back, his knife in one hand, his other going to his face. I hit him full tilt while he was off balance and we both crashed to the ground, me astride his chest. I grabbed his wrist as I felt more than saw the knife coming toward me. We were suspended for seconds that felt like hours in an arm wrestling match as we fought for the knife. I brought my other hand around and, using both my hands, smashed his hand to the ground again and again, until I felt his grip loosen on the knife. As the knife fell from his grip, he heaved me off him and we both scrambled for the weapon. I had landed on my back when he shoved me and I half turned as we both grabbed for the knife. It was in my hand and I was bringing it up as the guy jumped on top of me with his full weight. Between his momentum and my own, I felt the knife slide into the man damn near to the hilt. He went still and looked down at himself and I threw him off me and scrambled to my feet. The knife was sticking out of his belly just below his breastbone. I felt my blood run cold as I looked at the big wooden hilt sticking out of his chest. Almost in slow motion, he dropped onto his back on the ground, his face grey as the blood drained from his body into the sand, staining the ground around him.

"I didn't mean to," I told Kate. "He jumped on the knife." I could hear my voice rising, panic creeping in.

"It's okay, John, he would have killed you and raped me. He had to be stopped." Her voice had a note of hysteria in it, too. But she seemed to be a lot calmer than I felt.

"Yes." I was regaining control of my senses as the adrenalin returned to normal.

"You alright?" I took her chin, tilting her head to look at her throat where the man had held the knife, then I realized my own arm was covered in the guy's blood. My stomach lurched as I dropped my arm and quickly looked away. It wasn't the sight of blood so much as what I had done, even if by accident.

"I'm fine, John." She seemed much more composed than me. My emotions were racing between relief that we were both safe and a sick feeling in the pit of my stomach from knowing I had killed a man. Even though he had jumped on the knife, it was in my hand and what I had done was almost inconceivable.

"Let's get the hell out of here," I said.

She began repacking our noon dishes onto the horse, while I went to look at the man in the bushes. He was still on his back where I'd left him. I felt his neck for a pulse, but I didn't find one. I stood looking down at his lifeless body, feeling my stomach churn even more as I realized I'd killed two men.

"I'm just going to go wash my hands," I told Kate as I walked quickly past her. I hurried down to the river and scrubbed the blood from my hands, then I stood up quickly and threw up into the bushes. I stood there for a minute, leaning my weight against a tree, my head hanging, until my stomach began to settle. Then I went back to the river and kneeled down, washing the acrid flavor of death from my mouth. So much for that lunch. I shook my head sheepishly as I made my way back to Kate. She seemed so cool and composed, I sure wasn't going to tell her I had been tossing my lunch in the bushes.

She had picked up the man's rifle and tied it on her horse and, as I walked closer, I saw her brace her tiny foot against the greasy man's chest, wrench the big knife free and wipe the blood off it onto his shirt. She almost looked like a serial killer in a movie. Like she dealt with this kind of thing all the time and it was no big deal. I felt a little dizzy as I watched her and my stomach churned again, the acrid taste returning. Good thing I already lost that lunch, I thought grimly as I looked away.

CHAPTER 10

Kate was determined not to show how scared she had been. She could still feel the cold blade of the big knife against her neck. She could feel John's eyes on her as she pulled the knife from the man's chest and wiped the blood off it onto his shirt. Her hand trembled as she did it, but she didn't think John noticed. He seemed too busy dealing with his own emotions. She realized, probably better than he did, how close they had both come to death by the hands of those two ruffians. She knew for certain they would have killed John and, after raping her brutally, they would have killed her to keep her silence. Her stomach felt weak and ill as she thought about it. She hadn't been expecting John to react as quickly as he had. And the way he'd leaped on those men, fighting to the death for both their lives. His valor in the face of grave danger caused her to perceive him differently now. She sensed that in his time, fighting off bandits was a little more rare than in her own time. Even back in Ohio, things had been a lot more civilized than these untamed western territories. At least traveling with a wagon train, there had been many armed men to protect from marauding Indians and lawless bandits. She realized now how truly alone and defenseless they were out here. Thank God she had John with her and he'd come charging through the underbrush to her rescue.

"You did good back there," I told her when we were back on the trail.

"You did well too, John Baker. You saved both our lives."

"Yeah, I guess you're right." That made me feel some better, but my stomach still churned at the thought of what I had just done. I had never killed a person before. Hell, I hadn't even been in a fistfight since high school. I had never been in the military, I hadn't worked for the government, killing people with my bare hands. No, I was just a truck driver, and this brutal world she lived in was going to take some getting used to.

We walked along solemnly for a bit, each lost in our own thoughts. I couldn't get the two lifeless bodies out of my head. And the sight of that guy's blood across my arms, it would probably haunt my dreams.

"Tell me more about your world," Kate said after we'd walked in silence for a bit, both of us kind of in a state of shock. She probably just wanted to get our minds off the bloody battle we'd been through and truthfully, that was fine by me.

"My world is ruled by the clock," I told her. "Get up at a certain time, go to work at a certain time. Take a break at a certain time. I never realized it before, but our day to day lives in my time are completely organized and ruled by a clock. I think I like this way better. It's either daylight or dark."

"Tell me more about your machines."

"Do you know what a telephone is?" I couldn't remember when it had been invented. Like I said, history was never my best subject.

"No. What is it?"

"You can talk to people on the other side of the country or even the other side of the world."

"We can do that now, silly. It's called the Post. I mailed a letter to my aunt Rose when we stopped at Fort Laramie."

"Not quite the same, Kate. Imagine if you could pick up a handset and speak to your aunt right now, the same as you're talking to me?"

"Really?" There it was, the childlike wonder was back on her face, her big blue eyes stretched wide.

"Really. Nowadays, we even have a video phone, so that you can see the person you're talking to, and we have cell phones so that you have it with you everywhere you go."

"I really, really wish to visit your world, John Baker. There's not much for me here, anyway."

"If it were possible, I would take you there, but I just don't know. I'm not even sure how or why I ended up here."

"I told you, John. Providence brought you to me."

I stopped walking and pulled her close, kissing her long and deep.

"I believe you," I whispered, holding her tight. I didn't know if it was the talk of destiny or if I was just happy we were both alive after that harrowing experience, but I felt a strange contentment as I held her, the horror of what I'd been through fading quickly in her tiny arms.

We walked in silence for a bit, then I tried explaining computers to her.

"It's called the world wide web," I told her. You can type a message to anyone in the world and they receive it instantly; you can order products and have them delivered to your door instead of going out shopping, plus there's much, much more that computers do. They run our whole world in the future." Great, now I'm thinking of my own time as the future. I wonder if I'll ever see it again. Then another thought struck me, what if my describing the future to her could somehow alter events, like stuff I'd seen in movies? Maybe I shouldn't be telling her this stuff.

We camped that night on a rise overlooking the river. There were tall, brown grasses covering the hills and we had to clear a place to build a fire. We used up the rest of Kate's coffee and there was very little sugar left. She did, however, still have potatoes and flour. She showed me how to roll the dough and make biscuits in a frying pan.

"Delicious," I lied as I munched a biscuit. It's not that they were bad, they just weren't too good.

"We should be at the mission soon," she answered, as if she was reading my thoughts. "Hopefully, we can get a good meal and sleep indoors. It's getting too cold at night."

"It is that, and we're running out of food."

We had looked for Jeremiah's cabin as we followed the river, but we never saw it. We had been hoping for a night inside. This camping out had been quite an experience and I'd really enjoyed sharing it with her, but I sure was looking forward to a warm, dry bed and a roof over my head. And to think, she had been living like this for six months, and had walked most of the way across the country. Most people I knew would never have made it. Then I thought about her parents and the people from the wagon train they had buried along the way. I guess a lot of people didn't make it.

I unwrapped the cloth from Nip's feet after dinner and turned him loose to graze.

"I think he'll be alright now without wrapping his feet," I told Kate as I watched the horse graze. "He's moving a lot better."

"Yes, I think you're right."

After our sparse dinner, Kate brought a pot of warm water she'd heated on the fire and set it down in front of me, then began rummaging around in her pack.

"What's that for?" I pointed at her pot of water.

"I thought you might like a shave." She pulled a straight razor and a small hand mirror out of the pack.

"Yeah, my face has been really itchy," I ran my hand across the stubble.

I gave it a try with the straight razor while Kate held the mirror. My hand damn near trembled, I was that scared of the thing. I hadn't even seen a straight razor since I was a kid and I sure hadn't ever tried to shave with one. Kate finally took it from my hand.

"I can do it," she said. "I've watched my father shave with it many times."

I sat very still, afraid she would cut my throat, but she was surprisingly gentle and adept as she shaved my face.

"There," she said, holding the mirror up for me. I couldn't see much by the firelight, but I ran my hand across my cheek and it was baby soft and smooth again.

"Thank you," I said, wrapping my hand around her head and pulling her to me for a kiss.

"Aah, that's much better," she whispered, rubbing her face against mine. It was an intimate moment and I stood still, enjoying the closeness and her fresh autumn scent.

We finally sat down by the fire and I leaned back on my elbows and crossed my legs at the ankle. She leaned back into my shoulder and put her head on my chest. We stayed that way, quietly enjoying the beautiful night and each other until the fire died down and the cold air drove us into our blankets. It was cold and cloudy and the cold dampness of the ground seeped through my body, but yet is was such a simple contentedness, as I held Kate close to my body and stared into the dying embers of our fire. It was such a far cry from my old life; racing through traffic from one city to the next. If not for missing my family, I would've been perfectly content to stay right here with Kate forever.

CHAPTER 11

We got our first look at the Whitman Station the next morning. It was about midmorning when we topped a hill, looking over what seemed almost like a small village. There was a huge white house with a fence of upright logs around it. I thought I remembered reading somewhere they were called 'palisades.' On past it was another, smaller house and corral fences stretched between the two. The corral fence was built out of upright slabs of wood. The white house was much bigger than I had expected. From books and movies, it always seemed like everyone lived in small log cabins. This house was big and very pretty. We could see a mill and a mill pond past the houses and an irrigation ditch ran across in front of the whole property. I could see the autumn remains of a garden between the mill and the houses and dried-up flowers from what must have been a very pretty flower garden. There were white people and Indians moving about the property and there were fat beef cattle and horses grazing across the hills.

"We made it," Kate said.

"I'm impressed, I didn't think it would be this nice."

"Let's go." She started down the hill happily, leading her horse behind her.

I followed along behind, staring at this busy village before me. It's almost like watching history happening in front of me, I thought. It was kind of awe inspiring. I figured now I had the child-like wonder on my face.

We wandered up to the big house leading Kate's tired horse behind us. A tall man stepped from the door just as we arrived. "Welcome," he said to us. "I'm Joseph Kimball." He stepped forward and shook my hand.

"I'm John Baker and this is Kate Donovan."

He gave a slight nod in her direction. "My apologies for the lady of the house. Mrs. Whitman is upstairs, tending the sick. The immigrant house is yon." He pointed to the second, smaller house. "You are welcome to turn your horse into the corral or set him free to graze. There was a field past the mill where I could see several eastern-type horses and a bunch of fat Cayuse ponies grazing together.

"Thank you sir," I told him. I think we'll let him graze after we unpack."

We made our way over to the immigrant house, where I stripped the packsaddle from Nip and turned him loose. We watched him make his way across to the other horses, then I picked up the packs and we entered the house, eager to sleep in a warm bed for a change.

As we entered the house, we quickly saw that a warm bed was out of the question. It was a good size house, but it was filled with people. Entire families had pallets made out of their blankets along the walls. At least it's warm, I thought as we looked for a place to stow our gear.

A short, round lady left the big pot she was stirring in the fireplace and introduced herself. "I'm Mrs. Danbury," she said as she held out her hand. I shook her hand and was surprised at how warm it was. Must be the heat from the fire, I thought. Her cheeks had a rosy, warm glow about them, too. She took Kate's hand too, and held onto it as she led us to another room. "There's more room in the back bedroom," she said. We followed her to a bedroom, where we found more families lying about. I noticed that a lot of the children and some of the adults were coughing and sniffling. There was a bed in the room with a lady and two children in it. All three looked pretty sick to me as we passed by them.

We put our stuff against the wall and headed back outside. I didn't know about Kate, but I wanted to spend the least amount of time as possible around all those sick people. Place looks like a college dorm after an all-night party, I thought to myself.

"That sure was a lot of people in one house," I said to Kate when we got back outside.

"Yes, but I'm concerned about the sickness," she answered. "It may be measles, which is highly contagious."

"Measles. I think I was vaccinated for measles," I told her.

"Well, I wasn't."

I got quiet as we wandered the property, looking around at what these people had built here. I remembered a little from history class. Smallpox. That's what I remembered. Was it the same thing? I didn't think so, but I remembered how these diseases spread and killed so many of the pioneers and the Indians, too. I had a vague memory of reading about the pioneers bringing sickness that wiped out most of the Indians in these parts.

"What makes you think its measles?"

"We heard about it when we stopped here on the way west," she answered. "We didn't meet anyone with it before, but we heard about Indian children dying from measles."

"Damn, what are we supposed to do now?"

"I don't know John, I'm thinking."

We walked down to the mill pond and sat down beside it.

"Maybe we should go back and look for Jeremiah's cabin," Kate said at last.

"Yeah, and what if we still don't find it? It's getting mighty cold at night to be camping out." I looked at the date on my watch. November twenty-eight. December was not going to get any warmer.

"We'll just have to find it. I don't know if it's the sickness or what John, but my gut tells me we shouldn't stay here."

"Alright then, but can we at least stay the night? I was really looking forward to a roof over my head for a change."

"Yes, John, I was too." She looked over at me and smiled, but there was a worry line creasing her forehead.

We wandered around the area the rest of the afternoon. We followed their irrigation ditch back to the river, then walked through the herd of horses and cattle grazing across the hills. The fat Cayuse ponies were more wary of us than the Eastern horses, but most of them were curious as we made our way between them. Nip's head came up as we approached and Kate scratched his favorite spot behind the ears, then he went back to his grazing as we walked on. I thought about all the fences that would be here in my time. It was pretty cool to just set the horses free and let them graze.

When we got back to the immigrant house, Mrs. Danbury was serving up the stew she'd been cooking over the fire. We each took a bowl and shared a small settee to eat. It was a little old couch with a flowered cloth print and heavy scrolled wood along the back of it.

The kind of furniture that would sell for a lot of money back in my time.

It was a wonderful stew, with beef and potatoes and carrots. It reminded me of a stew my mother made when I was a kid. And we were both thankful to be indoors and eating a good hot meal for a change.

We turned in right away after dinner, unrolling our blankets and stretching out together on the floor.

I had thought I'd sleep good being indoors, but the moaning and coughing of the sick kept me up. One of the small children in the bed was begging for water sometime in the night. I had to go outside to a bucket with a ladle in it. I couldn't find a cup, but I did find a bowl someone had left by the fireplace. I filled the bowl and carried it to him.

"Thank you sir," the little boy told me after he'd emptied the bowl.

"You're welcome, young man." I tousled the little guy's hair, noticing a red rash on his face and spreading down to his neck. "Hope you feel better," I told him, returning to my place beside Kate.

Kate got me up before the sun had even risen the next morning. I felt like I'd only just got to sleep and I didn't want to get up.

"Come on John, we need to get out of here," the urgency in her voice woke me up and I slowly climbed out of my warm bed and began repacking our gear. I checked on the little boy in the bed as I passed by him. His face was so deathly pale, it made the red rash stand out against his skin. I couldn't actually tell if he was breathing or not. I leaned in for a closer look.

"Come on John," Kate hissed, poking her head back through the door. "Let's get out of here."

CHAPTER 12

Kate didn't know what had come over her. All this way to get here, and she had *so* been looking forward to a warm bed and visiting with Mrs. Whitman. Yet, from the time they arrived, a horrible feeling had been hanging over her, almost like a sick sense of dread in the pit of her stomach. She couldn't explain it to John, but the feeling stayed with her as they wandered about the property in the afternoon and it was there throughout the night as she tossed and turned. She heard John get up in the night and tend the sick child and she feigned sleep when he returned to bed. But, as she was falling back to sleep with John's arms tight around her, a small smile wrinkled the corners of her mouth as she thought about how sweet her 'future man' was to get out of bed and tend the sick boy.

The horrible sense of dread was still with her as she woke before dawn and she did her best to rouse John, determined to get away from this place of sickness and death.

I left Kate at the house while I went to fetch Nip. A heavy fog had rolled in overnight and when I stepped outside, I felt like I needed to put my hands out to find my way. Daylight was just peaking across the eastern hills, but it did very little to brighten the day. The fog was like trying to see through a misty soup. I made my way slowly across the hills where the horses had been grazing, but I found nothing. Between the dark and the fog, I couldn't see across the fields either. I tried calling out to see if I'd get an answering neigh from Nip, but I heard nothing.

I finally made my slow way back to the house and found Kate outside, waiting for me.

"I couldn't find him in this damn fog," I told her.

"Then we'll have to come back for him later," she said impatiently as she began repacking our gear. Now we would have to carry what the horse had been carrying. Although it was a lot lighter, since we were running out of supplies.

I was beginning to feel her same sense of foreboding. I don't know if it was the fog or the sickness in that house or what, but I felt it, too. We should get out of here. Chills actually ran down my spine as the thought lodged in my brain.

We carried what we could, leaving the packsaddle behind. I hated the thought of leaving the only horse we had behind, but I followed Kate as she lifted her heavy pack and set off into the heavy fog.

As the new day was breaking, we could see quite a few Indians milling around in the fog. More than when we'd first arrived. And they weren't busy working, more like just milling around. We walked on by them and set off the same way we'd come, beginning our journey back downriver.

The fog lifted as the day wore on and we stopped for lunch beside the river. We had cold jerky and water since we were out of coffee.

"I really hope we can find that cabin, Kate. I don't think we want to spend much longer out here like this. We're running low on supplies and we keep losing horses. With winter coming on, I'm afraid we're going to die out here if we don't find some shelter."

"I know. I was just thinking of how much my family left home with and what I have left now."

I hugged her to me and felt like a heel for complaining. She'd been through so much more than me, and besides, I'd jumped off a bridge and put myself in this situation.

"We can go to Fort Walla Walla if we don't find the cabin soon," Kate said. "I think it lies a ways north of the mouth of this river. Surely the soldiers will take us in."

"Okay then, at least it's something for a plan." I had my doubts about us finding the cabin *or* the fort in this wilderness. What if we just kept wandering around out here, until we either froze or starved to death? It was not a comforting thought.

It was afternoon when we heard a horse coming through the brush across the river. We stayed back in the trees and watched as a man led a horse down to drink. I felt pretty wary after the last encounter we'd had with men in these woods.

"Nip!" Kate screeched. She ran over to the river, jumped in and started wading across, holding her bedroll up on her shoulders. I had no choice but to follow, but when I hit the icy water, I almost turned back. "Son of a bitch," I mumbled under my breath when the water came up to my stomach. I looked up at Nip and saw the man jumping back on, bareback. Kate was already out of the water ahead of me and she grabbed the horse's rein. "This is my horse, sir," she said angrily.

"My apologies ma'am, but I'm riding to the fort for help. I just grabbed the first horse I could get my hands on. Haven't you heard what happened?"

"No. What happened?" Kate asked, some of her anger subsiding.

"There was a massacre at Whitman Station. The Indians," his voice rose excitedly, "they killed Doctor and Mrs. Whitman and several other people and they are holding captives in the Whitman's home."

My blood ran cold and I felt my hands begin to tremble as I thought how close we'd probably come to being murdered. Guess that explains the intuition Kate had, I thought to myself. I probably would have still been sleeping. "Why?" I asked him.

"I'm not for sure, but there's been a lot of unrest this season among the tribes. So many immigrants have brought sickness this year and many Indians have died, including a lot of their children. They just buried a small Indian boy at the mission this morning. There's been some whispering that they hold Dr. Whitman responsible."

Kate bowed her head at the mention of the children and her grip loosened on the rein. The stranger suddenly kicked the horse and yanked the rein, ripping it from her hand.

"I'll return the horse," he called over his shoulder, "or set him free and he'll find you." He galloped away before we could move.

I felt anger and helplessness as I watched him gallop away. Then I saw the pain and hurt in Kate's eyes and I pulled her to me.

"Don't worry, little one." I wrapped both arms around her and pulled her into my chest. "We'll get him back."

"It's not just Nip," she said into my chest, her voice quavering. "All those people at the Mission. And the Whitmans. You didn't get a chance to meet them, but they were wonderful people. I just can't believe they're gone."

"I can't either," I said dejectedly as I held her. *But I sure am glad we got the hell out of there.*

We built a fire to dry our clothes. The temperature felt like the high forties, I guessed. The sun was shining now that the fog had cleared, but it was still damn cold and we had to get dried out. I stared into the flames as I thought about what I'd gotten myself into. I could picture the soft couch and big-screen TV in my apartment. And here I was running from measles and from massacring Indians, facing freezing to death or starvation in this wilderness. I looked at the beautiful, tiny blond girl sitting across from me. I smiled as I looked at her. Yep, she's worth it.

"What could you possibly find to smile about?"

"I was thinking how warm and comfortable it would be back home, but how I'd rather be here with you."

"Oh, you were not, John Baker." She threw a pebble at me and I jumped up and chased her around the fire, both of us laughing ridiculously, until I caught her and pulled her to me for a kiss.

"We'll get through this, Kate." I said softly as I held her shoulders and looked into those big blue eyes. "I'm not sure how, but we'll make it."

"I know that, John. I have complete confidence in you."

"Well, I'm glad one of us does."

She giggled at that and I held her tight as I thought again about our narrow escape from the massacre.

We got ourselves dry, then continued on our way, sticking to the north side of the river. No use crossing back over through that icy water. We made several more miles that day before calling it quits. We were both unnaturally quiet as we walked. I'm sure she was thinking, as I was, about those poor folks at the mission and our own dire situation.

Kate had brought the remainder of our vegetables, which wasn't much, and we made a stew over the fire.

"I've gotta toughen up Kate," I told her as we ate. "I need to learn to use your weapons so I can hunt and I've got to figure out the old ways so we can both survive. I wish I'd paid more attention in history class."

"Old ways?"

I looked at her and we both laughed.

"Okay. *The ways.*"

She giggled some more at my joke.

"I used to go hunting with my dad, but it was more of a sport. We weren't going to starve if we didn't get a deer or whatever," I told her.

"Then what did you do for food?"

"We have grocery stores. You go buy what you need. We didn't have to kill it, butcher it and then cook it."

"Oh, that sounds nice. Is your family wealthy?"

"No, that's just how it's done in my time. My family has a farm and apple orchards in Washington. They've always done pretty good, but they're not rich."

"I can show you some stuff with the rifles, but I'm afraid I can't help you with hunting and such. My father would never have allowed it. Although, he did teach me to shoot pretty well."

"Then we'll learn together."

"Really, you don't mind if I go hunting?"

"No little one, you can do anything you want to do."

"Good, then I want to learn to ride a horse—like a man—astraddle. My father allowed me to ride some as a small child, but as I got older, he said it was not ladylike. He couldn't afford a sidesaddle, you see."

"Done," I told her, "as soon as we get your horse back."

The temperature dipped that night and we huddled together under both wool blankets, and I got up several times to keep the fire going, but it still wasn't enough.

We were stiff and chilled to the bone as we sat around the fire the following morning, not even a hot cup of coffee to warm our bones.

We heated the remainder of our vegetable stew on the fire, then set off in the frosty morning air. I was determined that we find some sort of shelter today, or else head straight to the fort.

We had walked several hours and we were thinking of stopping for a lunch of cold beef jerky, when I thought I saw a door hidden in the hillside. We walked toward it, and we could see rough-cut logs forming walls as we got closer.

"I think we found it," Kate said excitedly, grabbing my arm. "I think this is Jeremiah's cabin and we didn't find it before because we were on the other side of the river."

"Hmm...maybe." I knocked on the rough wooden door just to be sure, hearing nothing inside, but getting an ugly splinter in my hand. The door looked like thick wood, but I'd have to duck my head a little to go through it. The walls on each side disappeared into the hillside. The house was built literally into the hill.

When nobody answered, I finally lifted the crude latch and threw the door open, yelling out 'hello' as it creaked open. I could see a roughly-built table and benches sitting on a stone floor and a fireplace built of rock, but no inhabitants. Kate pushed past me and went inside, throwing her arms out and spinning around, laughing excitedly. "We found it, John. Now we have shelter; food will be our only concern."

"Yeah, I'll just make a run to the market. You want anything?" I joked sarcastically as I looked around. We surveyed the cabin, which didn't take very long; it was only the one room, there was what I assumed was a kitchen in one corner. No stove or sink, but a couple pots and pans hanging on the wall and a few plates, bowls and cups on a shelf, alongside two tall, tin containers. Kate looked inside and smiled, holding them out for me to look. One tin held coffee and the other, flour.

"Hallelujah!" I yelled excitedly. I never thought I'd be so happy to see ground coffee—such a simple, easily obtained commodity. I had definitely taken it for granted my whole life. The only other things in the room besides the table and benches were a bed in the opposite corner and a rug on the floor in front of the fireplace. Not a rug really, but an animal skin covered in brown hair. Deer, maybe? How the hell did I know from skins? The only window was beside the door. It had glass in it, but the panes weren't exactly clear, it was kind of like looking through a glass bottle. Being built into the hillside and with only the one small window made it pretty dark inside. I found a little firewood and some kindling and got a fire going in the fireplace. As I added logs and the fire crept higher, the small cabin was bathed in a warm, orange glow.

"What's this?" Kate was staring at the wall beside the fireplace, where a message had been scrawled on the rough boards with a coal from the fire. The firelight had lit the room enough now that I could see it too.

*To whoever finds this cabin, I leave
it in your stead. I won't be coming*

back as I have the consumption and
am going south where the air is better.
Theres food in the cold room out back.
Jeremiah Harding

"It is Jeremiah's cabin," Kate said. "I wonder why he didn't tell us the truth."

"Probably didn't want us to feel sorry for him."

"Hmpff." Kate sniffed, as if put out.

"Don't worry, little one, it's a guy thing," I chuckled. "I'm gonna go look for his food storage." I gave her a quick hug as I passed her and headed outside, the chilly air making me shiver as I wandered around, looking things over. It's no wonder we didn't see this place before. I stepped back and looked at the cabin. There was a layer of dirt across the roof with moss growing on it. It's a wonder that we saw it at all, buried into the side of the hill as it was. I found a path up the hill and followed it to the back of the house, where I found an outhouse off to one side and another little room buried in the hill on the other side.

Kate caught up to me as I pried open the heavy, wooden door. "Oh." She sucked in a breath and held it as we stared. We could see pounds of potatoes, carrots, wild onions and camas bulbs. I grabbed Kate, picking her up and swinging her around in my exhilaration. She giggled when I set her back on the ground.

"We're saved. Now I've just gotta kill some meat and we'll have everything we need."

"I'll go with you," she said. "I can show you how to use the guns as we hunt."

"Okay." I followed her back to the cabin, feeling very skeptical about my hunting abilities. We picked up our gear and carried it inside, and then I brought in more firewood from a small stack near the door. Another task I'll need to attend right away. Damn, can't we just call the landlord and say the furnace is broken? I really just wanted to lie down in front of the warm fireplace and do nothing for about a week.

Kate untied her rifle and the one I'd taken off the scoundrel who attacked us, lifted them free of my pack and then, handing one to me, she set off at her tireless pace. Sighing heavily, I followed along, hoping we could kill something quick and hurry back.

CHAPTER 13

We walked for a couple of hours, not finding any game whatsoever, when Kate suddenly stopped, sat down on a log and showed me how to load my rifle. I hadn't known it while I walked, but her rifle had been loaded and mine hadn't.

"What if we'd seen a deer?" I admonished her.

"You know I can shoot, John Baker."

I did know that. I'd seen her shoot, but I still felt foolish, knowing I had been carrying around an empty rifle.

"These rifles are very dangerous if you don't know what you're doing." She showed me how to pour in the black powder, tapping the butt of the gun on the ground to shake the powder down, then she put a ball and wadding into the muzzle and tamped it in with a ramrod. Next she pulled the hammer back to a half-cock and inserted the cap. "The ball has to be seated against the powder or it could blow up in your face. And you want to always keep it at half-cock until you're ready to fire."

"Yeah…um…okay." My mind was reeling from all the information and from watching her load the gun. The steps were confusing and I didn't know if I'd remember the correct order. Slapping a clip into a pistol, I understood. All the steps she'd went through were pretty confusing.

"Maybe I'll just throw these knives at the animals. I don't trust your ancient weapons." I picked up the smaller knife, flipping it in my hand and threw it by the blade, watching in amazement as it stuck into a tree.

"Why didn't you tell me you can do that," Kate sounded as amazed as I felt.

"Lucky throw, I guess. I was just playing around."

"You should practice this talent. You never know, it may come in handy."

"Okay, I will." Feeling proud of myself now, I walked over, pulled the knife from the tree and, stepping back, I flipped it in my hand again and threw it just like I did the first time. We both watched as it bounced off the tree, hitting the ground at the base of it.

"Told you, lucky throw."

"You just need practice," she answered.

I tried it again and again, occasionally sticking the knife into the tree, although never as well as the first throw. I tried it different ways but never really figured out what I was doing wrong. It still seemed more like chance when it actually hit the mark, but I found I was enjoying the challenge and I decided I'd stick with it.

"Let's head back since we're obviously not going to get any meat today," Kate said, rising from the log and picking up the rifles.

We started back, me carrying my now loaded rifle, holding it out in front of me with both hands, like it was about to explode. Kate giggled as she watched me.

"Sorry," I chuckled too. "These black powder guns are a lot different than the rifles I grew up with. I don't trust them."

We wandered along quietly for a bit, the only noise was from my too large boots as I crunched across twigs and tripped over vines. Kate seemed to move almost soundlessly through the woods. She looked almost as if she floated along silently in front of me, her long dress almost touching the ground. I knew I had a lot to learn if I was ever going to be any good at this woodsmen thing.

I was watching where I put each foot, trying to move as quietly as Kate, when I saw a movement out of the corner of my eye. We had scared up a rabbit from the undergrowth and Kate had brought her rifle up and fired before my mind had even registered the fact of what I was seeing. She ran ahead of me and picked the bloody rabbit up by the hind legs, holding it up in the air for me to see. The muzzle loader had put a hole through the chest of that bunny that I could damn near see through.

"I killed it, so you get to skin it," Kate said happily.

"Holy shit, really? Can't we just order a pizza instead?"

Kate giggled as she turned and headed back the way we had come, carrying the dead rabbit upside down by the hind legs.

We got back to the cabin and Kate showed me how to remove the guts and skin the rabbit. She held it up by the back legs while I skinned it. I had been starving all day, but now I really didn't feel very hungry anymore.

"I'm going to go wash my hands," I told her as she headed inside with the rabbit.

"Don't be too long, I'm starting dinner," she held up the carcass and I felt my stomach roll. It looked like a large, hairless, headless rat.

I hurried down to the river, where I kneeled and scrubbed my hands repeatedly. I was air drying my hands and staring into the river, trying to see my reflection and, when I looked up, I was staring into the eyes of a deer on the opposite side. She stood deathly still, staring back at me with her big, brown eyes. I hadn't brought the rifle, but I still had the knife I'd been throwing. I slowly picked it up by the blade, never taking my eyes off the deer as I rose. And then...I wussed out. I was afraid I would do nothing more than hurt her with my small knife. I turned away, giving her one last look and headed back up the rise to the cabin.

Kate had already started a rabbit stew over the fire, using some of Jeremiah's potatoes, carrots and onion. The smell of the stew already enveloped the small, warm room and I felt my stomach growl, my hunger quickly returning. I gave her a kiss, and then went back outside to chop enough wood for the night.

Inside the food storage building, I found an ax, a small shovel with a narrow blade and various other tools I didn't recognize on a shelf. I picked up one with a round wooden handle and a pointed blade like an icepick. "Hm, I'll have to ask Kate if she knows."
I grabbed the ax and went back through the small door. There were several dead trees along the side of the hill that Jeremiah had felled, but hadn't yet chopped. I set to work and I could feel the burn in my chest and shoulders as I swung the ax, over and over until I had at least enough wood to get us through the night. I made a few trips to the cabin, carrying as much as I could with each load. By the time I was done, Kate had dinner ready.

CHAPTER 14

Kate's rabbit stew may have been the best meal of my life. My stomach had settled as I worked and I was literally starving after all the hard work and activity. She had made a big pot of stew and yet, we finished it off, sitting across from each other on the hard wooden benches

"So…What do you think?" She asked as we ate.

"About what?" I said around a mouthful of stew.

"About this cabin? What are the odds of us ending up here?"

"You're thinking its providence?"

"Aren't you?"

"I hadn't really thought about it at all, but you're probably right. We were going to either starve or freeze to death if we didn't find something soon. God looks out for fools and little children. That's what my dad always said."

We built up the fire and turned in after dinner, both of us looking forward to sleeping in a real bed with a roof over our heads. We crawled into the bed and the softness of the mattress was unbelievable. Jeremiah had used goose and duck down to make a feather bed. I folded Kate's small warm body up into my chest and was instantly asleep.

I woke up the next morning to the smell of baking bread and the sounds of Kate bustling about the cabin. I lay still with my eyes closed, contentedly taking in the sounds and smells. When I finally crawled out of the warm bed, I saw that, along with the baking biscuits, Kate was boiling a large pot of water over the fire. "What's that for?"

She pointed to a large, round tub in the middle of the cabin. "I'm going to clean this cabin today and do laundry and you go do man things, but first...a bath. If you would please help me pour the hot water?"

"Sure." I found a cloth to use as a potholder and poured the hot water into the tub for her, seeing that she had already added some cold water to make a decently hot bath.

"Now strip out of those dirty clothes," she told me.

I looked at her to see if she was joking. She looked pretty serious, so without giving her a chance to change her mind, I stripped off my clothes and stood before her in all my nakedness.

"Now you." I know I must have had a gleam in my eye as I watched her undress in front of me. She removed her clothes hesitantly—maybe even shyly, staring into my eyes the whole time. She had thin shoulders for such a strong girl, small perky breasts and a tiny waist. My gaze traveled all the way down and then back up to her eyes. I saw an impish sparkle in her ice-blue gaze this time.

"Into the bath," she told me, her voice gone husky.

I turned and sat down in the small tub, crossing my legs Indian style. Even then I barely fit, but the hot water felt incredible.

Kate took a cloth and a bar of soap and proceeded to bathe me. It was a new experience for me and it was completely erotic and sensual. I closed my eyes and relaxed as she ran the cloth over me. She even washed my hair and I tilted my head back as she poured clean water over my head to rinse it. When she was done, she brought a sheet and wrapped it around me since we didn't have towels.

I emptied the water out the door and we poured fresh for Kate. She insisted on washing her own hair; it was so long I probably would have only made a tangled mess of it. But I did bring clean water and poured it while she rinsed, then I picked up her cloth and bathed her, enjoying every minute of it. I started kissing her before I had even finished, then finally I picked her up out of the tub and carried her, still dripping, over to the bed.

After our morning's lovemaking, I set off to chop wood and try my hand at hunting again. I whistled happily as I worked and, after I had chopped wood for about a half hour, I brought out the small knife and tried out my throwing techniques again. I threw the knife again and again at the tree I was chopping and I seemed to be improving. I was beginning to figure out how to get it to stick into the tree and I began working on my aim, trying for the same spot each time. It seemed to be a matter of balancing the knife correctly in my hand before I threw it. It seemed to work better when I held it by the blade. I practiced flipping it in my hand and catching it by the blade before throwing it. I kept at it for a while, then went back to my wood-chopping. Once I had a stack along the front wall of the cabin almost as high as the window, I quit for the day and went inside for Kate's rifle.

"I'm gonna go kill something," I told her jokingly, making my voice as deep and gruff as possible.

"Okay, tough guy, just be careful with that gun," she said, kissing me lightly on the lips.

CHAPTER 15

Kate smiled to herself as she worked about the cabin, sweeping and dusting everything in sight. Even though she didn't have much experience being with a man, she was sure that she and her 'future man,' as she thought of him, had something very special. Her heart felt as if it might burst from her chest when she thought about their passionate lovemaking, his ability to make her laugh, and even how handsome he was. He had a boyish charm that she really enjoyed and she still hoped that she could return with him in the spring to the year two-thousand and ten. The thought of seeing so far into the future excited her almost as much as John did.

"I love you, John Baker," she said to the empty cabin. Do I dare say it to him? What if he doesn't feel the same? Her thoughts continued on this path as she heated more water and refilled the tub for her laundry. She scrubbed their spare clothing with the bar of soap. Then, moving the two wooden benches in front of the fireplace, she draped their clothes over them to dry, her mind filled with thoughts of love. She used the water left in the tub from her laundry to scrub the stone floor, working her way slowly across the small space as she thought of John. Would she have a future with her 'future man,' or did destiny have a different plan in store for them? No, surely he wasn't sent back through time for her, only to return to his own time without her. Not if she had anything to say about it!

CHAPTER 16

I followed the river downstream, holding the rifle out in front of me, still in the half-cocked position she'd shown me. I still didn't trust it, but I was beginning to get used to the feel of it. The barrel length was much longer than modern rifles and it was much heavier. I had used rawhide strips to strap the two knives to my leg, but I didn't carry the powder to reload the gun. I wasn't sure if I'd remember how to do it correctly and I wasn't interested in having the damn thing blow up in my face.

The knives kept slipping down my leg and I constantly had to readjust them. I tried tying the rawhide strips tighter, but then it damn near cut off my circulation. I had also tied some of the rawhide strips together, then tied one end to the rifle barrel and the other end to the stock of the gun, thus forming a sling so that I could carry it over my shoulder.

I came upon a few Canadian geese and some ducks out on the river, but I went right on by. I figured if I did scare them up, I'd probably miss with this gun and even if I got one, I didn't want to leap into that icy water to retrieve it. I moved as quietly as I could through the woods, watching where I put each foot so as not to step on twigs or loose stones.

I had walked about two hours and then sat down to rest, leaning my back into a tree on a slight rise overlooking the river. The river was narrower here and rushing across the rocks; it made a beautiful sound and it was really the only sound out here. No traffic, no horns, no people. I relaxed and closed my eyes, setting the rifle down on the ground beside me. The sun slanted through the trees and warmed my legs where it fell across them.

I must have drifted off for a bit because, when I opened my eyes, I didn't remember where I was at first. I stared at the river in confusion for a couple seconds, then as an image of Kate swept across my vision, I remembered exactly where I was.

I stood up, stretched, and figured I'd better head back. If nothing else, I'd take a shot at one of those geese I'd seen. I picked up the rifle and started around the tree, looking up the hill behind it. I was thinking to climb up out of the trees to make for easier walking, when two deer came to the edge of the hill and stopped. They were looking at the river and sniffing the air. Looked like a couple of young bucks—fork horns—my dad called them. As they began making their way down the hill, angling slightly away from me, I slowly raised the rifle to my shoulder and took aim on the closer one. I held my breath and slowly began squeezing the trigger and…nothing happened. Damn! I'd forgotten the half-cock thing. I lowered the rifle slowly and pulled the hammer back to full-cock and eased it back to my shoulder. I was afraid they were getting out of range now so I quickly squeezed off my shot. Son of a bitch! It felt like that damn gun ripped the ligaments loose in my shoulder. I saw the first deer take off out of there like his ass was on fire. The second one leaped in the air and fell down, but was on his feet and running before I could lower the gun. I took off after him, following a trail of blood through the undergrowth, my shoulder on fire from the kick of that big gun. The deer was moving upriver, out of sight of me, but there was a pretty good blood trail to follow. I tracked him for about a mile before I found him. He was down but scrambling, trying to regain his feet. I set the empty rifle down and pulled the big Bowie knife loose from where it was strapped to my leg. I jumped on the deer and rammed that knife in his neck as his head came around, trying to stick me with those short antlers. I brought the knife down, slitting his throat and severing the artery. I jumped back as the blood poured. The deer was down for good now. I wasn't sure if I felt proud of myself or sickened by the kill. We needed the meat, I kept reminding myself. I made sure it was dead, then gutted it and, picking up the rifle, I grabbed the deer by the antlers and started dragging it toward the cabin with one hand, the rifle over my shoulder. I was out of breath in about ten paces. I stopped, staring at the deer, thinking. Finally, I unlashed the knives from my leg and, taking the rifle from my shoulder, I untied the sling I'd made. I tied the leather thongs together, then tied them around the deer's neck. I then tied the other end of the leather straps around my waist. Now I had to carry the rifle and two knives, but it was easier than trying to drag a hundred pound dead weight with one hand. It was over a mile back to the cabin and up and down hills.

My legs felt like rubber by the time I arrived. I drug the deer up near the cabin and collapsed on my back beside it. Kate came out the door and I grinned as I heard her gasp, but I kept my eyes closed for a minute while I rested in the warm sun.

"I'm just resting," I told her.

"I thought for a minute you and that deer had killed each other," she said as she sat down beside me, fluffing her skirt out around her daintily.

"I kinda feel like it too." I sat up and pulled her into my lap, kissing her hard on the mouth. "But I did it. I brought home the dinner."

"Now we just have to skin it and butcher it."

I groaned at the thought. "Just let me rest a minute first."

"I'll see if I can find some rope or something to hang it by while you rest up." She jumped off my lap and headed to the storage room in back while I lay back down beside my kill. I was damn proud of myself now that the nasty killing part of it was over. I'd seen my dad shoot and dress out deer when I was young, but I'd never actually shot one myself.

Kate came back a few minutes later with a piece of rope she'd found in the shed and carrying the ax I'd been using to chop wood. I lay still and watched her throw the rope over the limb of a tree and tie one end to the deer's hind legs. God, but this woman is amazing. So sweet and tender one minute, so tough and strong the next.

I jumped up when she handed me the ax and she directed me in removing the deer's head. Then, when she began pulling on the rope to lift the deer into the tree, I reached over her and, grabbing the rope above her small hands, we both heaved until the deer was hanging upside down from the tree. I tied our end of the rope off to the trunk of the tree, then we began the work of butchering the deer.

"Do you want to keep the skin?" Kate asked.

I hadn't given it any thought, but now it set my mind to racing.

"Do you know how to tan hides?" I asked her.

"I only know a little from my father, but he never let me help. Those two Indian boys told me their tribe soaks the hide in deer brains and hot water."

"Ugh. That sounds really gross."

"I guess the brain oils soften the hide for making their buckskin clothing."

"Well, let's keep it then and I'll give it a try. We could certainly use the clothing." I only had the two sets of her husband's clothes and my pair of pants I'd arrived in. I didn't really expect any of it to last very long with this rough lifestyle. I'd already caught my pants on a tree limb and torn a hole in them.

We carried the skinned deer to the storage room and hung it from a rafter along the back wall, the coolest area of the room. I went back out to deal with the brains and skin, while Kate cut us some venison steaks for dinner. I took the ax and split the skull of the deer, removing the brains into the washtub, which was the only thing I could find to put them in. Next, I picked up the skin, trying to figure out what I could hang it on. I remembered the icepick-looking tool I'd seen in the shed and I headed back around the cabin, where I met Kate as she was coming out the door with her venison steaks.

"Hey, do you know what this tool is?" I picked it up off the shelf and held it out to her.

"It's an awl...for making holes in leather."

"Aah. Should work." I took it with me back to the skin and used it to make several holes around the edge of the skin. Through these holes I inserted pieces of the rawhide string and then, stretching the skin between two trees, I tied it to various limbs with my rawhide string.

"Not bad," Kate said when she returned. She instructed me on scraping all the flesh and fat from the underside of the skin. I went after it with the blade of the knife for a couple hours, until Kate called out the door.

"Dinner's ready."

"I'll just go wash up first," I called back. I looked at my hands, there were bits of flesh and fat and blood everywhere. I just hope I can figure out what I'm doing, I thought as I stared at my hands.

I cleaned up and went in to dinner. The smells in that warm little cabin almost knocked me down when I opened the door. The bread, the vegetables, the steaks— oh, beautiful venison steaks—I felt like I could eat the whole deer right now. Must be the fresh air. I sat down on one of the hard wooden benches and Kate set a filled plate in front of me and a hot cup of tea. Never in my life had I been so grateful for these basic necessities…food, warmth and a good woman to share it with.

We curled up on the animal skin rug in front of the fire after dinner, warm and full and comfortable. I stretched out on my side, and Kate curled up into my chest.

"Tell me more about your family," she said.

"My mom is short and round and strong, but the sweetest, most lovable woman you would ever want to know. She has a quiet, classy wisdom that I've always admired. She worked the farm and orchard right alongside my father and still made time to raise three rowdy boys. She was determined that we be raised with the proper manners and etiquette. She taught us to dance and play piano. I always thought of it as if she were trying to tame wild horses."

Kate giggled at the thought. "And your father?"

"My father was strict and strong, but at the same time warm and loving. He kept us boys busy working on the farm, but he also loved to take us fishing and camping, and a night out for dinner and a movie was a weekly family affair. Good times." I stared into the flames as my mind traveled into my past, which ironically, was now in the future. "They found him a couple of years ago, out in the orchard. His heart had given out and he died out there, doing what he loved."

"I'm sorry," Kate said quietly.

"My brothers," I said with a lighter tone, "on the other hand, were the wild ones. I was the youngest and I could hardly keep up with them. They were constantly playing jokes and pranks on me, on my mother, on each other. They were horrible little devils. Actually, we all were."

"What did they do?"

"Well, we had a tire swing hanging from a tree. We would swing out over the river, then let go and drop into the water. My brothers cut part way through the rope. Then, when I got on the swing, they got it swinging and gave me a pig push. I landed all the way across the river in the bushes and brambles while they laughed their asses off."

Kate laughed too and sat up to look at me. I stretched out more and leaned my head on my hand as I talked. "I got them back, though. The oldest, Brad, I opened a can of tuna and hid it under the seat of his car...in the summertime. After a few days, the whole car smelled like dead fish."

Kate's eyes lit up as she laughed and her face had a happy, relaxed look.

"The other one, Jake, I waited in the bathroom til he was pounding on the door, then I put superglue on the toilet seat. He was in there for a while. I had left a new magazine in there for him. When he stood up, he ripped off some of his ass hair. You could hear his howl of pain throughout the house. Probably a good thing I didn't put much glue, or he woulda been walking around with a toilet seat attached to his ass."

"Oh, that's horrible! But you're family sounds wonderful."

"They are. I really miss them. I didn't even think about it when I jumped off that bridge. I bet they found my car and I know a guy saw me jump. I bet it broke my mother's heart. I wish I could go back and tell her that I'm okay and that I'm happy here with you."

"You are?"

I stared into those beautiful ice-blue eyes. "Of course I am. It may be harder times here, but it's also a simpler, cleaner, better place than in my time. No smog, no factories polluting the air and water. This area seems so clean and pure now. The air is so fresh, the water is crystal clear and full of fish. I think the world would have been a better place without the progress men have made."

"But you said you were happy here with *me*?" Her gaze was intense now as she stared at me.

I took her small hand and pulled it to my chest, keeping it in my larger one. "I've had lots of girlfriends in the past and a few that I thought I was in love with," I told her.

"Yes?"

"I did love them, but now I know that I wasn't *in* love with them."

"How do you know that now?"

"Because now...now I know what it's like to fall head over heels, madly in love with someone."

Her eyes grew shiny as tears welled up.

"I think you were right about providence, Kate. Maybe God sent me here to show me what I still have to live for." I don't think I'd ever opened up to anyone like that before and if she didn't feel the same, I didn't think I could take it. "I think we're soul mates, Kate. I think you're the one I've always been searching for." I moved her hand on my chest over to my heart. "This belongs to you now." I kept my hand over hers where I held it on my heart.

Her tears spilled over now and I watched as one rolled down her cheek. I leaned forward and kissed it away, followed by a passionate kiss on her soft lips. She responded in kind and I was surprised when she pushed me down onto my back and, straddling my waist, she ripped her dress off over her head. We made love for hours right there in front of the fire, until we were exhausted and she fell asleep in my arms.

CHAPTER 17

I don't think I've ever been this happy in my life, Kate thought as she lay nestled in John's arms, staring into the flames. When John had professed his love to her, she'd felt her own heart slamming against her chest. He'd stared into her eyes with such love and passion and, when he kissed her, she'd let go of her senses completely and pulled her dress off over her head. She wondered as she was falling asleep in his arms, if he would ask her to marry him and, if so, where would they be able to find a preacher out here in the wilderness? She snuggled against his broad chest as he wrapped both arms tight around her. She drifted off to sleep, happy and secure in John's love.

CHAPTER 18

We woke up late, still in front of the fire, which only had a few glowing coals left. I slipped my arm from under Kate's head and added wood to the fire. As the fire grew and the firelight played off my naked skin, I looked down at myself. I knew that I'd grown leaner since I woke up in her wagon, but I really hadn't had time to give it much thought. I could see now that every inch of my body had transformed into taut, lean muscle. I ran my hand down each arm, across my shoulders, even down my legs. Every muscle was firm and hard like an athlete. Just like those two Indian boys. All those hours of chopping wood and walking had turned me into a different man. It felt good to get my body into the shape of an athlete. I had always been in pretty decent shape, or at least, I had thought I was. I thought about how much money was spent in my time on diet pills and gyms. All those folks really need is to go out into the wilderness and work your ass off to survive. I smiled smugly as I threw on some clothes and headed out to the shed to cut off some venison for breakfast. I had never been more content and happy with my life than I was at this moment, here with Kate.

There was a morning mist hanging along the river. It looked eerie and ghostly, yet peaceful and serene. I stopped as I made my way back to the cabin and took in the beauty of it, the fresh, clean air and the absolute silence. Never in my life had I known such peace, such sheer, unadulterated happiness.

Kate woke up when I went back inside and I watched her stand and stretch, the firelight dancing off her naked body. It froze me in my tracks and I forgot what I was doing. I still had the steaks in my hand and I was about to throw another log on the fire, but as I stared at her splendid nakedness, I almost threw the steaks into the fire instead. I caught myself in the nick of time and picked up a log, tossing it on the fire as I grinned sheepishly.

I cooked breakfast for her and we ate in front of the fire, still giddy from the most passionate night of romance I had ever known. Lucky for her she had gotten dressed, or it would have continued right through the morning.

"I love you, John Baker," she said softly as we ate. I reached over and touched her face with the back of my hand.

"I love you too, little one." I stared into her eyes. She had a warm, gentle glow to her amazing blue eyes this morning. I almost felt like I could see my soul in them, as if I could drown in the deep, blue depths of them.

After breakfast, I went back to my morning routine of wood chopping and knife throwing. I decided to try the knife throwing first, before my arm got tired from swinging the axe. I tried moving in closer to the log I'd been throwing at. I tried twenty feet, then fifteen. I found that at fifteen feet, I could hold the knife by the handle and get it to rotate a full flip and stick into the end of the log. I tried it again and again, hitting the mark every time. I moved back to twenty feet and tried again. The knife bounced off the log and, frustrated, I tried again and again. Finally, a thought struck me, what if I held the knife by the blade. I flipped it around and, aiming as I did before, I watched the knife rotate one and a half flips and stick into the log. Perfect. I retrieved it and tried it again, and again, hitting the mark each time. Now I was getting a hang of the distance versus blade rotation.

"You're getting really good."

I was so absorbed in my practice, I didn't know she had even come up behind me.

"Its progress. I think I'm getting the hang of it." I wrapped an arm around her and gave her a kiss, then put the knife in her hand. "You give it a try." I moved her closer and instructed her how to aim. She hit the target on her first try.

"I did it, I can't believe it."

"You did good."

Kate tried it a few more times with no luck, then gave it up for the day. I kept trying to show her how to extend her arm, but she insisted on girl throws, with her arm too limp. I practiced for about an hour, improving more and more as I tried out different distances, and then went back to chopping wood.

We had more of the deer for lunch, and afterward I went back to the skin I was drying. I was able to scrape the underside better now that it had dried out some, but it was still a messy job. I removed all the hair from one side and the remaining bits of fat and flesh from the other side. I was left with an unidentifiable skin, similar to the one in front of the fireplace, but without the hair. I took it down and added it to the tub with the brains. I started a fire in the yard and boiled water in the tub with the deer brains, using a stick to stir the brains in like a soup. "Ugh, brain soup," I said as I stirred, smiling to myself. I had to look like a witch out there, stirring my potion over the fire with a stick.

While the skin was soaking, I went about building a frame to stretch it on. I used more of the rawhide strips to tie my frame together and leaned it against the cabin wall. It was really no more than poles forming a square, but it should work, I hoped.

When this was done, I built another frame in the middle of the yard, burying the upright poles so that it was standing. I built a new fire under it, using green wood to create more smoke. Then I went to the shed and cut strips off the deer, hanging them on the frame over my fire. I was hoping I could learn the art of making jerky since we had no freezer for our meat. I kept a small fire going under it the rest of the day, flipping the venison on the rack occasionally.

I pulled the deer skin from the tub before dark and stretched it out on the rack I'd built, making more holes along the edge with the awl and tying it tight with the rawhide string. I pulled the strips of venison off the smoker rack and hung them back in the shed. I seemed to have achieved more of a smoked meat than jerky. I cut off a small piece and tried it. It was good, it had a nice smoky flavor. Maybe it just required longer smoking to make it into jerky? I figured I could throw it back on the rack tomorrow to find out.

Kate had made a venison stew for dinner, with potatoes, onions and carrots and one small biscuit for each of us. It was wonderful after my day of labor. The cabin was warm and cozy with a small fire going in the fireplace.

"We haven't seen another human since we found this cabin," I said to Kate over dinner. "It seems like we're the only two people on Earth."

"I know. I rather like it myself."

"Me too." I didn't think there had been a day in my life that I hadn't been surrounded by people. This solitude was a nice change and I was enjoying the challenges of learning how to survive.

"I would like a bath after dinner, John. If you would be so kind as to scrub the deer brains out of our washtub?"

"Sure," I said. "Sorry. I couldn't find anything else to put them in."

Kate boiled water in the washtub after I cleaned it and we took turns bathing in it. We got cleaned up and turned in early, cuddling together under the blankets.

The next morning, I started my fire and put the strips of meat back over it. I stretched my deer skin tighter on the frame, poking at it with my fingers, trying to test the drying process. If I had the internet, I could figure this tanning process out in a minute, I thought wryly. It didn't seem to be drying very well with the chilly, damp days we'd been having. I moved the frame over by the fire and leaned it against my smoking rack. I didn't know if the smoke would be too good for it, but I figured the heat from the fire should help dry it out.

I picked up the big Bowie knife and tried throwing it at the log. It had a very different feel and balance than the smaller knife. I wasn't sure if I could even use it as a throwing knife, but I figured that, other than breaking the blade, it couldn't hurt to try. After a few tries, I managed to get it to stick, now I just had to figure out what I had done. I tried it again, bringing the knife up by my head, blade pointing at the sky. I gave a flick of my wrist as I threw it and watched in amazement as it hit the mark. It had a razor sharp blade and a curved point, but it was pretty thick metal. It stuck pretty deep into the end of the log. I wondered what it would do with some precision and force behind it. I tried it over and over, hitting the mark more than missing. I practiced with both knives for an hour, stopping occasionally to feed my smoldering fire. It seemed as if I was improving more every day and if nothing else, I was enjoying learning how to throw the knives.

I went down by the river and cut some small willows and carried them back to the yard and stripped the leaves from them. I found Kate's piece of net we'd used for fishing and tied it around the willows, forming a big square. I took the rope we'd used to hang the deer and threaded it through the net, far enough down from the opening so I could pull it tight, closing off escape for any fish I might catch.

Kate had lunch ready by then and I went inside. She had washed our other set of clothes and was using the benches for drying racks. We took our plates and sat on the floor in front of the fire to eat.

"Mmm. Venison again. Good choice," I joked.

"You know we have to eat it before it spoils."

"I know. Do you know much about making jerky?"

"You must remove all the moisture from the meat. And it may help to rub salt into it before smoking."

"Aah, I'll try that. Would you mind keeping my fire smoking this afternoon while I go fishing?"

"Sure John, I don't mind."

"Are you okay?" She didn't sound like her usual happy self.

"Yes, I'm fine John Baker. Just a little tired maybe."

I felt her forehead with the back of my hand. "You're a little warm. Maybe you should lie down and I'll wait on the fishing."

"No, I'm fine. You go ahead."

"If you're sure?"

"Yes, I'm sure."

I pulled her to me and held her small body tight for a bit, her thin shoulders seemed even more thin than before, almost frail.

"Maybe you're working too hard. Why don't you take it easy today?" I told her.

"I will John." She stood on her tiptoes and kissed me, her lips soft and warm.

I went out the door and added a bit more wood to my fire. I strapped the two knives to my leg, picked up the fish net and headed to the river. I walked about half a mile before I found what I was looking for. The water was shallow and rapid here, moving quickly across the rocks. There was a large boulder sticking out of the water, it ran from the middle of the river down about ten feet, slanting in toward the bank. There was a deeper pool between the boulder and the bank. Perfect spot, I thought. I cut more of the willows and, wedging my net between the rock and the bank, I drove the willows into the muddy bottom to hold it in place. I drove another willow through the back side of the net to hold it upstream, then climbed out of the freezing water and sat on the bank, holding my rope. If my idea worked, when any fish swam through my net, I could pull the rope tight and trap them. I sat still for about an hour, holding my rope loosely as I gazed around. The absolute serenity of this place was so relaxing, I was feeling like kicking back for an afternoon nap. I could see a little ways into the cold, clean water. When two big salmon swam into my net, I could see their movement and the water swirled as they fought the net. I yanked my rope tight and started hauling it in as the weight of the fish pulled the willow sticks free. I got the two fish onto the bank and chopped their heads off and gutted them, leaving the remains behind for the wildlife. I put the fish back into the net and slung it over my shoulder for my hike back. I had forgotten to tie the big knife back on my leg and I didn't want to set my fish down so I carried it in my hand.

I had walked for a ways when I scared up a rabbit. It ran about twenty feet, where it froze as soon as I stopped. It was just in front of a dead log with a bunch of willows and undergrowth behind it. I knew if I took a step it would be gone. I brought the big knife up slowly, the blade pointing toward the sky, then quickly threw it. As I released the knife, the rabbit leaped as if it was going to jump over the log. The blade went all the way through it and stuck into the log. "Son of a bitch," I said out loud. I could only stand and stare at the dead rabbit, pinned to the log. "Why couldn't I have a camera... or video, that would be even better," I mumbled as I pulled the knife from the log, unpinning the rabbit. Nobody back home would ever believe me, not that I expected to ever be able to tell them. I threw the rabbit into the net with the fish and continued on my way, whistling happily.

CHAPTER 19

"Look what I caught," I yelled proudly when I threw open the cabin door.

Kate was covered up in the bed, shivering, and I saw that the fire had gone out. I dropped my catch on the floor and ran to her. She was burning up with fever and moaning. I tore off a piece of the old sheet, soaked it in our drinking water bucket and placed it on her forehead. She hardly seemed to know I was there as she moaned from her pain and fever.

"Kate," I said softly. She opened her eyes and looked at me, but she quickly closed them again as she moaned softly.

I rebuilt the fire and carried the fish and rabbit back outside. I worked quickly, worry for Kate making my stomach hurt. I didn't know if she had a cold or flu or what, but I knew how sickness had claimed so many lives back in this time.

I skinned the rabbit, washed it and cut it up for a stew. I brought a couple potatoes and an onion from the shed and added everything to the pot, hanging it over the fire. I hung the two fish up inside the shed, thinking I'd deal with them tomorrow when Kate felt better, hopefully. I took her a bowl of my stew and a hot cup of tea, but I couldn't get much of either into her, although she seemed a little cooler now and more coherent.

"Do you have any kind of medicine?" I asked her.

"Laudanum."

"Laudanum? What the hell is that?"

"It's a tonic," she answered, setting down her cup and dropping weakly back into the pillows.

I searched around the cabin and found a dark brown bottle on a shelf in the kitchen. It said 'Tincture of Opium' and in smaller letters underneath, 'Laudanum.' It had a skull and crossbones in red under the words. Mother of God, what are these people taking? I carried it to her and she uncapped it and was about to take a swig when I stopped her. "Just a tiny sip," I told her. "I don't trust that shit."

She did as I asked and I put the bottle back on the shelf in the kitchen, out of her reach. If she overdosed on opium, it wasn't like I could call 911.

I took the bucket to the river and brought back more of the ice cold water. I dipped the piece of sheet in it and put it back on her head. She fell asleep again right away, whether from the fever or the harsh drug, I didn't know.

I sat up with her all night, changing the cloth every few minutes. She didn't wake up all night, but she moaned in her sleep and tossed and turned, the fever burning her up from within, and I knew it was probably causing aches and pains throughout her body.

She seemed a little better by morning, her face was cooler and her eyes were brighter. I reheated my stew and she ate a small bowl.

"It's good," she said, her voice quiet and hoarse.

"I'm glad you're feeling a little better," I said, brushing the blond hair back off her forehead. "I was worried about you. I hope it's just one of those twenty-four hour bugs." I sucked in a breath and cold chills ran down my back when I saw the red rash spreading from her hairline down to her neck. Just like the little boy at the mission, I thought. "I think you might have the measles," I said quietly as I caressed her arm and shoulder. "Do you know how to treat it?"

"No. We have nothing except the Laudanum, anyway."

I sat with her until she drifted off, and then I went outside to my chores. The weather was cold and breezy and the sky was overcast with low-hanging clouds, but I got my fire going again anyway and continued smoking the strips of deer. It seemed to be working, however slowly. I worried for Kate as I worked, and I opened the door quietly every little bit to check on her, but she hadn't stirred. From the stories we'd heard, and what I knew of these diseases wiping out so many of the Native Americans, I had an uneasy dread hanging over me like a shroud as I worked. If she got sicker and sicker, would I be able to help her? Or was the worst behind us? She *had* been much better this morning. She'll be fine, I kept telling myself as I worked. I cut the fish into strips, rubbed salt across the meat and hung the strips on the rack over the fire.

Then, I picked up the Bowie knife and practiced throwing it for a while, only missing occasionally. I seemed to have a bit of a knack for throwing knives and it was a hell of a lot better than having that damn musket blow up in my face. I was still thinking about my throw the day before with the rabbit, and feeling proud of myself, but worry for Kate overshadowed my glory.

I removed the deer skin from the drying rack and took it inside. It seemed to have dried out thoroughly now. I sat down with it by the fire and examined it. One thing was for sure, it wasn't going to become a soft buckskin shirt. It was much too stiff for that, but the tanning process seemed to have worked pretty well otherwise. I took the big knife and split the skin down the middle, wrapping one half around my foot and leg. I thought it might make some decent moccasins if I could figure out what I was doing. I pulled out Kate's sewing kit and, choosing the largest needle and thickest thread, I began sewing the hide where the pieces came together on top of my foot. The leftover pieces I cut into strips to make more of the rawhide string.

I stopped occasionally to feed my smoking fire outside. My fish seemed to be smoking pretty well, although it was kind of a funky smell coming off the smoke. Might work better with the proper wood for smoking, I thought.

I finished sewing one moccasin together and tried it on; it came to just below my knee. It was a damned unattractive job, but it seemed like it would work. And God knows, I needed something better than her dead husband's boots. Not only were they a little too big, but the soles were wearing completely through. The poor guy had already walked damn near two thousand miles by the time I got them.

Kate woke up and I went over to her as she stirred, still wearing my one new moccasin. Her fever had flared again. I took her a drink of cold water and put the cold, wet rag back on her head. She was soaked with sweat and sick on her stomach and I could see more of the red rash spreading across her skin. Cold chills ran up my spine as I looked at her and I mumbled a bit of a prayer as I went to fetch the medicine. I gave her another small sip of the Laudanum and she soon slipped back into her fitful sleep. She moaned occasionally as the fever soared. I brought the bucket of cold water inside by the bed and kept soaking the rag in it, holding it on Kate's face and neck.

After a couple hours of it, she felt a little cooler to my touch and I went back to my chores. She had never awakened, but she seemed to be sleeping more comfortably.

I went back out into the twilight to take the fish off the rack and hang them back in the shed. When I opened the door to go out, I saw my fire had long since died and there was a damn raccoon hanging from the rack and stealing my fish. "Get out of here," I yelled as I ran out the door. That little dude jumped off the rack and took off before I could reach him, but he held on to the strip of salmon he'd stolen. "Little bugger," I mumbled as I took the rest of the fish to the shed.

I spent another hour making my second moccasin and then wore them out to the shed while I fetched deer and potatoes for a soup for Kate. They felt very comfortable after those stiff, oversize boots, but I could feel every stone and stick through the soles. I looked around in the dark for that little thief of a raccoon, but I didn't see anything. I made sure to pull the door shut tight on the shed when I left. The last thing we needed was that little bandit stealing what food supplies we had.

Kate woke up a while later and I was able to get her to eat a little soup and drink some cold water. "It's good," she said, her voice raspy with a sore, raw throat.

"Can I make you a hot tea?" I offered as I held her hand and kissed her hot forehead.

"No, just more Laudanum please," she begged. I gave her another small sip, then returned the bottle to the shelf in the kitchen. "Where did you get those?" She croaked out when she saw my new moccasins.

"I made them." I posed for her, turning this way and that, and standing like a model on the runway, until she giggled through her pain.

"Good job," she said weakly, then she dropped back into the pillows and groaned softly. Her face was red from the fever and I could see the red rash spreading down her neck and onto her chest. It looked really ugly and my stomach churned as I stared at it. But what could I do to treat it? I remembered the salve she'd put on my feet when they were blistered and I went searching for it. I dug through her pack and finally found it, buried underneath her mother's jewelry box. I took it back and applied some gently to her face and neck.

"Oh, that feels better," she mumbled. "It was itchy and burning, but that really helped."

"My poor little one," I said as I touched her face tenderly and smoothed the hair back away from her forehead. "I wish there was more I could do for you. I would gladly take your sickness onto myself if I could."

"Thank you, John Baker. But I'll be alright. I'm sure of it," she lied.

CHAPTER 20

Kate had told John she was sure she'd be alright, but she wished she felt as confident as she'd sounded. She was sure it was the measles, as she knew immigrants and Indians alike had been succumbing to the disease this season. She felt the fever burning her up from inside. It racked her body with pain and her head hurt horribly, although she didn't tell any of that to John. She could feel blisters inside her mouth which made eating painful and her stomach was so nauseated, she really didn't want to look at food anyway. Just sleep; she begged for sleep, the deep, dreamless sleep where she knew nothing nor felt nothing. The laudanum tonic at least seemed to help her sleep. Once again, as she felt the drug making her groggy, she thanked God for sending John to her. She just hoped she survived this illness, so that they might enjoy the rest of their lives together.

CHAPTER 21

I took the bucket to the river for more water and Kate was out by the time I got back. If nothing else, I think the Laudanum helped her to sleep more comfortably.

I sat up with her most of the night again, keeping the cold rag on her head and bathing the ugly red rash. I didn't know if what I was doing was helping or not. I so wished my mom were here. She would know just what to do. Kate's fever seemed to be raging and the salve seemed to have made the rash uglier and redder. I had been up for most of two days and nights with her and I finally had to stretch out in front of the fire, sometime late in the dead of night. I got a little rest on the cold stone floor in front of the fire, but I was up instantly in the morning as Kate stirred and groaned. She seemed a little better again and her face felt cooler. I made her more soup and some hot tea, then I went outside when she drifted off to sleep again. I split more of the logs with the ax and practiced throwing both knives for a while. After a couple hours outside, I looked at the bottom of my new shoes. It seemed like the rocks weren't bothering my feet as much and when I looked at them, the soles were crusted black with the dirt and getting stiffer the more I wore them. Hmm, guess that's how they get the hard soles. Dirt.

I took more of the deer and potatoes inside to make more soup for Kate and I cut off some steaks for myself. There wasn't much left now; I was going to need to go hunting again as soon as possible. At least for now, I still had the fish I'd caught. At least what was left after that damn little masked bandit stole what he wanted.

When I went back inside, Kate was moaning and tossing in her blankets. Her fever was raging again and she seemed delirious when I reached her. She thought I was her father or her husband or someone. She said some stuff that didn't make sense, but she hadn't even opened her eyes. I tried putting the cold cloth on her head, but she kept pushing it off. She was shivering in the blankets, yet her skin felt like it was on fire. I tried for a while with the cold cloth and I even tried to get some of the Laudanum into her, but nothing worked. She seemed to be only getting warmer and warmer as her fever raged and she was so out of it, she didn't even recognize me when she did open her eyes. Her face was red and her eyes were bloodshot as she stared right through me. I tried and tried with the cold cloth. Either she pushed it off with her delirious thrashing or, when I could keep it on her head, she was so hot the cloth grew warm almost instantly. I was so frustrated, and so scared for her, I gave up finally with the cloth and, throwing the blankets off her, I picked her up out of the bed as she fought me. I don't know who she thought I was in her delirium, but she twisted in my arms and beat weakly at my chest with her small fists. I ignored her flailing fists and pitiful groans and carried her outside.

CHAPTER 22

I walked with her to the river, her small body so hot, it felt like my arms were burning where her skin touched me. It seemed like the fever was eating her from inside, like a fiery demon had taken over her body and was burning her alive. I waded right into the freezing water and sat down, holding her on my lap. I held her body down in the icy water for maybe ten minutes, only her head and shoulders above it. She had quit struggling and lapsed into unconsciousness as the ice-cold water purged the fire within her. I talked to God as I sat there, my legs going numb from the water. I prayed, I begged, I think I even cried a little, 'cause I was pretty damn sure I was about to lose her. She was just so small and limp in my arms. I put my ear on her chest, listening for a heartbeat. It was faint, but I could hear it. I shook her a little, trying to illicit a response. Nothing. Her face had gone from the fiery red to a ghostly pale and I'm not sure which scared me more. I carried her still form back to the house when she seemed cooler. She was so small and light, even soaking wet I don't think she weighed over a hundred pounds. I talked to her, I touched her face, I even tried yelling at her and pinching her arm, but she responded to none of it. I stripped off her wet dress and wrapped her in the blankets. Her skin felt better to my touch now and her shivering had stopped, but she still hadn't regained consciousness.

I cooked my steaks and started the soup for her, checking on her every few minutes. I watched her as I cooked and tended the fire, eager for any slight movement from her. Her fever was still down and the red rash looked a little less ugly, but she still hadn't moved or stirred. Her face still had a ghostly pallor that scared me more than the feverish red I'd seen for days. I watched her while I ate and while I stripped out of my wet clothes, changing into the other set of her husband's clothes, which she had washed and dried and folded for me before she became ill. I ate as an automaton. I knew I needed the nourishment, but I didn't taste the food. I racked my brain, searching desperately for any home remedies my mother had used, but I came up empty. Getting that fever down was what I knew had to be done, and I seemed to have accomplished that. But her pale, unconscious state was well outside my expertise. She needs a hospital, was the only thing I could come up with.

I talked to God some more before I curled up in front of the fire. I don't think I had said a prayer since I was a kid, but they were all coming back to me now. In this age of killing and sickness and death, I begged God to spare her life. She had never regained consciousness and I could think of nothing else I could do.

Finally, exhaustion took its toll on me and I lay down. I slept fitfully on the hard stone floor, a couple of hours at a time, checking on Kate every time I woke. Her skin felt cool to my touch and her breathing was slow and even, but she had still never awakened. I was sick with worry for her and still racking my brain for anything I could do to help her.

I woke up again, cold and stiff on the stone floor with a pale streak of light shining through the window. When I sat up, I was staring right into Kate's ice-blue, beautiful eyes. They looked clear and her skin felt cooler to the touch when I went over to her and put my hand on her forehead. I brushed the blond hair away from her face and ran my fingertips softly across her skin.

"You're feeling better?"

"Yes. Much." Her voice was still weak, but at least she'd regained consciousness.

"Can you eat?"

She nodded and I went to the fire, building it up to reheat her soup. She didn't eat a lot, but I did get some soup and cold water into her. The rash looked less red and angry today and her eyes seemed brighter and more alert. I was pretty sure that sitting in that icy water with her had done the trick to finally break her fever.

I had a talk with The Big Guy again while I cooked, thanking him for sparing this special, tiny woman who had stolen my heart.

After she had eaten and fell asleep, I set off on the hunt again, carrying the rifle and both knives. I even brought the powder and ramrod, trying to cover all my bases to get us more meat. I was afraid to leave her, but we only had a little of the fish left after that bastard of a raccoon stole part of it. We had to have more meat to get through the harsh winter ahead of us. I headed upriver this time, back toward the mission, keeping my loaded gun at half cock. I chewed on some of the deer jerky I had made as I walked. Not bad, a little tough maybe, but not bad. I had only gone maybe a half mile, my new moccasins helping me move quietly through the woods, when I surprised a deer drinking from the river. I pulled the hammer back and brought the rifle up as he took off away from me. I took a quick aim and fired at the ass of the fleeing deer. I saw it drop and I ran after it before it could get away. It was down when I got to it and I grabbed the big Bowie and quickly slit its throat, then went about the job of field dressing it. It looked like the ball had gone right through his ass and into his gut. I had brought the rope this time and I was busy tying it around the deer's antlers when I got the creepy feeling of being watched. I looked up the hill to see two big grey wolves staring right back at me. Their lupine heads were lowered, their tales wagging slowly, almost ominously. When I looked behind me, two more were circling to come up behind me. I didn't know if it was me or my kill they were after, but I quickly unstrapped the small knife from my leg and picked up the rifle to reload it. I watched them creeping closer as I poured in the powder and wadding and dropped in the ball. I grabbed the ramrod and started ramming it down when one of the wolves up on the hill leaped toward me. I brought the rifle up quickly, pulling the hammer all the way back in one swift motion and fired with the ramrod still sticking out of the barrel. The wolf was still in the air when the ball hit it, knocking it to the ground with the ramrod sticking straight up out of its side. It was a totally bizarre sight, but I didn't have much time to dwell on it as I saw from the corner of my eye, one of the wolves behind me was on the move. I could hear it growling as it moved toward me. I picked up the Bowie and threw it as I spun, catching the first wolf attacking from behind me right in his chest. He yelped and went down with that big knife sticking out of his chest and lay still. Now I was down to one small knife and a wolf on each side of me. I stood sideways over my deer, where I could keep an eye on both of them at the same time. The one on my right hadn't advanced after I shot his buddy, but the one on my left was creeping closer, a low growl coming from his throat, his head lowered and big teeth bared. I gauged the distance and, as it approached stealthily, I flipped the small knife in my hand, so that I was holding it by the blade. When that wolf jumped, I released the knife. It twirled through the air and looked like it was going to miss and, if I had been a second slower or the wolf a second faster, it would have. As the wolf rose into the air, the knife sunk deep into his belly. He yowled and dropped to the ground, where he tried to crawl away, a low whine coming from him. I looked back at the wolf on my right. It kind of danced and whined on top of the hill, but it hadn't moved any closer, so I ran and pulled the Bowie from the chest of the dead wolf and stabbed it into the neck of the one crawling away. I put an end to his pain as I slit his throat and I watched as his life force drained across the ground around him, painting the dirt a sticky red. I retrieved the small knife from his belly and wiped it on his fur, leaving red streaks across the grey coat. When I looked back up the hill, the remaining wolf was gone.

CHAPTER 23

Kate got better and better over the next few days and I fed her all the fresh deer and vegetables I could get her to eat. Her color was returning along with her appetite and the red rash faded a little more every day. I made her stay in bed as much as possible; the fever had weakened her and when she tried to do too much, her face turned white and I thought she was going to pass out.

"Good food and rest, Kate," I reminded her every day. "That's the only way to get better."

"Yes John, I know," she said every time as she ignored me and stubbornly went about her cleaning and cooking.

I set about smoking more venison and tanning another hide. My skills were improving with making jerky and I stored the finished pieces in the coolest part of the shed. Now that Kate was feeling better, I brought the remainder of my smoked salmon and some camas bulbs inside for a nice dinner. I even made a couple biscuits for us and we sat down in front of the fire to eat. Kate had tried to take over cooking, but I had adamantly refused.

"I'm just not used to seeing a man waiting on a woman this way," she said.

"Well, get used to it You still have to get your strength back and until then, you will be treated like a princess."

Kate smiled at that, her blue eyes sparkling. It was almost like a candlelight dinner as the firelight danced across her eyes. Even in her pale, unwell state, I thought she was the most beautiful girl I'd ever seen.

I told her the tales of my adventures with the wolves and how I had pinned the rabbit to the log.

"You're becoming quite the woodsmen, John Baker," she said.

"Mountain Man. That's what we called them back in my time. The men from this time who lived off the land and trapped beaver. They wore buckskin clothes and had grizzly beards."

"You're getting some of that yourself." She reached out and ran her hand across my scruffy face.

"Yeah, guess you'll have to help me take care of that later," I said, staring into those beautiful eyes.

"Thank you for taking care of me, John Baker."

I reached over and ran my fingers through her hair lovingly as I described how I sat in the river with her, watching her icy blue eyes sparkle as I talked.

Finally, I stood up and held my hand out to her. "Would you care to dance?"

She put her tiny hand in mind and I pulled her to her feet. "I don't really know how," she said, kind of nervously.

"Just follow my lead," I told her as I put my arm around her waist and pulled her close. I hummed a tune as I led her in a slow dance and then even sang some of it as she caught on to the steps.

"This is nice," she whispered into my neck as we moved together around the cabin. "You're a good dancer."

"You can thank my mother," I whispered back. "She was determined her rowdy boys would have some social skills." I showed her how to Waltz and Fox Trot and even to Tango, which she really enjoyed. Then I pulled her close again and we slow danced around the small room. I sang softly in her ear as we moved together. I sang an old love song from my high school days and finished by dipping her backward in front of the fire. Her girlish laughter filled the room—and my heart.

We danced until we were exhausted and then made love slowly and passionately in front of the fire. I thanked God again before I fell asleep for sending me back through time to be with this beautiful, amazing woman. And for saving her; from what I felt sure, was death from the measles.

CHAPTER 24

Kate listened intently to John's story of carrying her to the river and sitting with her in the water. She felt sure she wouldn't be here now if not for him. Then as he pulled her close and sang softly in her ear as they danced around the room, she felt her heart swell with love for him. He was so tender and romantic, she actually felt cold chills run down her spine. Never in her life had she known such a man as this. He was more than she could have ever dreamed of. He was virile and tough and fighting off wolves one minute, and twirling her around the room the next. He was masculine, yet so romantic. He had an impish gleam in his green eyes and she found his shaggy, unkempt hair adorable. In this world or his, she didn't care which anymore, she only knew she didn't want to live without him.

CHAPTER 25

My watch had the date on it and if it was correct, it was almost Christmas. I cut down a small fir and we decorated it as best we could, hanging jerky and Camas bulbs from it. It was comical, but these were precious items here, where our next meal could depend on what we could kill. I used my second deer skin and made her a pair of moccasins. That was the best I could do for a gift for her. But thanks to my improving skills, they did come out softer and prettier than mine. And a whole lot smaller. Honestly, I've seen children with larger feet. She was such a petite, beautiful little pixie girl.

She gave me a thin rawhide strip on which she had tied a cross from her mother's jewelry box. I kissed her neck and made her giggle while she was tying it around my neck. We sang Christmas Carols and I taught her some of the newer ones. She knew some of the old ones already, Silent Night and Rudolph the Red-Nosed

Reindeer. But some of the stuff she'd never heard, like Rocking around the Christmas Tree. I danced with her and sang it as I twirled her around the room. She loved those newer ones that she'd never heard and I taught her every one I could remember. She learned quickly and we sang them together as we danced around the cabin and sat by the fire.

"Merry Christmas," I whispered into her ear as I held her by the fire after we had exchanged gifts.

"Merry Christmas, John Baker," she whispered back as a tiny tear slid from her eye. It may have been simple and homemade, but it was a joyful Christmas in our secluded little cabin, locked away from the rest of the world.

I went hunting again the week after Christmas. The weather was getting colder and colder and we'd even had a little snow. I was afraid we were going to run out of food and I wouldn't be able to find any more.

And I was right. I didn't see anything as I wandered errantly mile after mile through the woods. It was as if the cold and snow had driven every living creature into hiding.

I tried my fish trap again and finally caught one big salmon after two days of trying. We still had a little of the deer left and most of the jerky I'd made, but I hoarded it away. I was too worried about the dead of winter still to come.

As we moved into the New Year, a cold snap came upon us and we spent a few days inside by the fire. A heavy fog had moved in and froze with the low temperatures and the world outside turned to ice. Tree limbs bent low to the ground under the ice and occasionally, we could even hear a crack in the forest, as a limb gave way and snapped off under the icy weight. Every surface had a coating of ice, every limb of every tree, every blade of grass was frozen stiff. The moisture from the fog had frozen our world, turning it into a crystalized fantasyland.

I went back on the hunt after a few days, even though the cold weather held. I didn't have gloves or a heavy overcoat, but I was watching our meager food supplies dwindling, and frankly, I was worried. There didn't seem to be any animals moving in the cold and ice and, every day, my search felt a little more desperate. I crunched through the woods across the ice, wearing the oversize boots again, at least until the ice melted. I walked for miles in each direction, my bare hands hurting from the cold, but finding no animals moving in this frozen world. I tried my fish trap again, my hands turning red from the icy water, but to no avail.

Kate, on the other hand, had such a happy-go-lucky attitude, she seemed completely unconcerned. "You'll find something, John Baker," she said every day when I came back empty-handed and dejected.

We rationed the rest of the deer and made soups out of it to make it last. Kate would only add two potatoes and a little meat so the soup was really lacking on ingredients, but it was better than nothing.

I finally caught a salmon just as the deer was running out. I smoked it in the fireplace and we had enough to get by for a few days if we were careful, but I continued the hunt every day. I hunted in the morning and fished in the afternoon, having no luck with either.

Finally, one day as I set out to hunt, I took the musket and headed downriver. I ranged further than I had before, determined to not return again empty-handed. The cold spell was still on us and the sky was low and gray and heavy. I was cold and hungry, but damn determined.

As I moved through the trees along the river, I heard a splash and saw the movement of an animal jumping into the water. I moved slowly toward it and I stopped behind a tree when I saw a beaver dam in the river. There was a gravelly island in the middle of the river and the beaver had built his home between the island and the river bank nearest me. I knew he must have jumped in and swam underneath the dam when he heard me coming. I sat down behind the tree and balanced the gun on my knee with the barrel poking past the tree toward the dam. I sat absolutely still in that uncomfortable position for what seemed like hours, until finally I heard a small splash just out of my sight on the bank. I held my breath and didn't move and sure enough, the beaver came waddling up the bank toward me. I let my breath out slowly as I squeezed the trigger and saw the beaver drop. I ran to it and picked it up by the tail. "Sorry Mr. Beaver, but we gotta eat too," I said as I headed back, my stomach growling as I thought about the hot meal we'd have tonight.

The meat from the beaver was a little tough and had a really wild, gamy taste to it. Kate turned it into a stew with a couple of potatoes. I can't say it was the best stew I ever had, but neither of us complained. We stretched the stew out over several days, eating small bowls with each meal.

With our appetites sated, Kate asked if I could show her more dance moves. I sang to her as I twirled her around the cabin, whatever songs came to mind, she loved them all. I held her close as we slow danced; I showed her moves I had learned in clubs with previous girls. I waltzed with her until we were both exhausted. Her eyes glittered as we collapsed by the fire. "It's so much fun, John. Thank you for teaching me."

I stood up and bowed deeply to her. "It's been my pleasure, my lady."

She laughed at my antics and rested her head on my chest as I stretched out on the floor. I had my hand resting on her flat stomach and she picked it up and held it in both her hands as we lay there. She seemed to be examining one finger at a time and I closed my eyes, enjoying her light touch as she went from finger to finger. "Your hands have grown work-hardened and calloused," she said as she rubbed her small fingers across my palm.

"Hmm," I groaned for an answer, enjoying her touch too much to break the spell. Her small hands worked their way up my arm to my shoulders, massaging, caressing with her fingertips. As they reached my chest, I grabbed her arms and pulled her down on top of me, kissing her long and deeply. The taste of her mouth caused me to groan again and I ran my hands down her back, wrapping them around her tiny waist. I could see the fire in her eyes as she sat up and pulled the pale blue dress off over her head.

CHAPTER 26

The next day I got lucky and scared up a deer. It was bedded down under some bushes and it hopped out right in from of me, giving me a perfect shot with the old musket. I tied the rope around its neck and drug it home, happy to know we had plenty of food again.

"See, I told you, John Baker," Kate said when I arrived with it. "You're a good provider and you learn quickly."

I grabbed her with one arm and pulled her to me for a kiss, reveling in her praise. She made me feel more of a man than I ever had in my life. She helped me skin the deer and we hung it in the shed, cutting off a couple huge steaks for dinner. There were still a couple of the Camas bulbs left and we roasted them in the coals also.

The following morning, I set about tanning the deer hide, using the brains as I did before. I was really hoping for a nice buckskin shirt this time. I could just envision it, me wandering through the woods, wearing a buckskin shirt with fringe hanging off the arms, carrying the musket and wearing my moccasins. I'll be a regular old mountain man. I had even let my beard grow out for a short time, but Kate didn't like it and who was I to argue with a woman with a straight razor in her hand.

I started a small fire under my smoking rack and cut off more strips of the deer. I was getting pretty good at making jerky, and at least it was something to eat if we ran out of food. I could see Kate as I worked, doing laundry down by the creek. She was squatting down with her dress fanned out around her, her small hands red from the cold water. She must have felt my stare because she looked up and gave me a huge smile. It was cold and cloudy out there, but I swear her smile brightened the day.

When she turned back to her task, I leaned one arm on my smoking rack as I looked around at what we had here. The small, cozy little cabin built into the hillside, with its chimney made of rock and its stone floor. Kate kept that one room so clean, even the stones of the floor were spotless and shiny from her scrubbing. It was a hard life, but as I stood there looking around me, I could imagine myself spending the rest of my life in this place, living off the land with an amazing woman by my side. I felt euphoric as I looked at what we had here, a sense of bliss at seeing our hard work provide for our simple needs. I thought about the life I'd left behind and the girls I'd known. Certainly none of the ones I'd known would have ever made it out here. Up to this point I had really only been intent on survival, living one day at a time, but as I stood there I contemplated the future and what we should do. I discussed it with Kate that evening as we had dinner by the fire.

"What do you see in our future? Do we stay here and live off the land or what?"

"I've been thinking about it, John, and I think it would be nice to continue on to the Willamette valley in the spring. There's plenty of good farm land for the taking, I'm told. That is, if you're willing?"

I scratched the stubble on my chin as I considered it. Give up my mountain man status to be a farmer? "Well I guess I could still hunt and traipse through the woods, *and* be a farmer."

"It'll be wonderful, John Baker, you'll see. It's supposed to be the Garden of Eden."

I had a good laugh and watched her face redden. "I *have* seen it, little one. Who told you it's the Garden of Eden?"

"The newspapers in the States. They run a new column every week, urging people to go west and settle the new land."

"Hmmph," I snorted. "It's definitely a wonderful valley with a great climate and rich farmland, but I haven't seen Adam and Eve running around wearing fig leaves."

"So, can we go in the spring, John? I would like to see my parent's dream realized."

"Sure, little one. I would love to be a farmer with you in the Willamette. Maybe we can even make a trip over to the Pacific."

Her eyes got really wide and sparkled as she said, "really John? I've never seen an ocean before."

"Then you shall see it, madam," I said royally as I made a sweeping bow and kissed her hand while she giggled.

CHAPTER 27

I still didn't get my buckskin shirt. I don't know what I was doing wrong, but the hide was just not coming out as soft as it should. I made a belt instead, drawing it tight around my waist with thin strips of rawhide poked through each end. It wasn't much of a belt, but my pants were damn near sliding off my hips with the weight I'd lost. I also made a sheath for the Bowie knife with a flap that tied it around my new belt and a rawhide string through the bottom end, to tie it around my leg. At least now I wouldn't have to strap it to my leg, it had been either constantly slipping down or cutting off the circulation in my leg. With the remainder of the hide, I made a sheath for the small knife that fit just inside the top of my moccasin. We spent many nights working by the firelight. Kate mended the holes we'd worn in our clothes while I worked at the sheaths. It was a quiet, relaxing time that we spent together in front of the fire and I began looking forward to it after a hard day of labor.

I practiced drawing both knives from the sheaths every day, pulling each one out and throwing it, all in one fluid motion. I got better and better until I could even stand with my back to the log, pull the knife and throw it as I spun around.

We still danced at night if we weren't working on other projects. I sang to her while we danced around the room. She preferred the oldies. She called them my future songs—which was ironic—most of them came from before I was born. I grew up with my mom singing to herself as she worked around the house and I guess a lot of the lyrics stuck with me. Kate had become quite the dancer and she would often spin away from me while I sang or hummed a tune. The pale blue dress billowed out around her as she twirled around the room, appearing as if she were floating. She seemed almost ethereal to me as she floated around the small space, her long blond hair cascading down her back, a small, secret smile on her face and those ice-blue eyes twinkling with joy. It was our own private Utopia, our refuge from the world. They were good times, in that small, one room cabin, and ones I knew I would never forget.

As January faded into February, we began running low on meat again and I set off on the hunt. The camas bulbs and flour were long gone. We had only a few potatoes and still a decent supply of tea and coffee. The weather was mostly cold and wet and miserable and I don't know where the game went in the winter, but they sure were scarce. I hunted every day; I tried my fish trap again and again, finally catching one small trout, which was enough for us to split for dinner. We rationed the rest of the deer, making it into soups and stews to stretch it further. We still had the jerky I'd made and if I didn't get meat soon, we'd be down to nothing else. One thing I was sure of, no matter where we were next winter, I planned on having a good supply of food set aside.

It started snowing one day while I fished. Big, soft flakes falling gently through the trees around me. I stopped what I was doing, holding my fish trap in the water's edge while I looked around. The silence was so absolute, it almost seemed as if I could *hear* the flakes falling. Big white flakes drifted lazily down between the trees, turning bare limbs white as they landed. It really looked just like a postcard as I watched the ground and trees slowly turning white.

I finally turned back to my trap, where I had been about to stake it into the mud, and damn if a trout hadn't swam into it while I had been daydreaming. I quickly pulled it onto the bank and stabbed the fish with the big knife, killing it instantly.

I got to my feet quickly when I heard a low growl behind me. I spun around, Bowie knife still in my hand. I stood face to face with a grey wolf. It was about thirty yards away in the unbroken snow and I looked behind it and then over my shoulder for the rest of the pack, but there was nothing. I wondered if this was the wolf whose pack I'd killed. When I looked back at it, the wolf whined and licked her lips as she stared at my fish. I bent down slowly and picked up the fish, never taking my eyes off her. I continued scanning the area too, in case she was here as a decoy while other wolves snuck around behind me. She whined again as she stared at the fish, but she wouldn't come any closer. I felt bad for her, she was skinny and hungry. I finally tossed the fish toward her and she leaped back as if I'd shot at her. I took my trap back to the river and, after I'd replaced it in the water, I looked back up just in time to see her grab the fish in her mouth and high-tail it out of there. Poor thing, I shook my head as I reset my trap. I bet she's the one that ran off when her pack attacked me.

I did catch two small trout that day, but Kate would only cook one. "We'll have the other one tomorrow," she said firmly. We had already been down to one meal a day, now we were even cutting that down. I looked down at myself when she wasn't looking. I had lost so much weight, my ribs were starting to show.

I dreamed of the lone wolf that night. I was standing in the river, catching fish with my bare hands and when I looked up, the wolf was standing on the river bank, waiting expectantly. As I threw a fish to the wolf, I could see a bridge off in the distance with cars crossing it. I knew I was back in my own time in the dream, but where was Kate? I had a sense that she wasn't there with me and I tore myself free from the dream, sitting bolt upright in the bed, instantly awake.

"You alright?" Kate mumbled sleepily.
"I'm fine, just a dream," I whispered and, laying back down, I tucked her small hand into mine and held it tight for the rest of the night.

CHAPTER 28

I continually hunted and fished every day and came home empty handed. I traipsed for miles through the wilderness, growing ever hungrier as I walked.

We were now down to a meal every other day and not a big one at that. I had never known hunger before in my life. Not real hunger, where there's a constant ache in your stomach as you search for food. The constant walking and hunting only served to increase the hunger pains. I even kept an eye out for that lone wolf. I figured she'd make a meal if it came down to it, but she had disappeared as well. I finally caught a decent size salmon in my trap one day and I smoked most of it, to make it last as long as possible. Still, we only had a meal every other day, and not a big one at that, and I continued hunting and fishing from morning until evening. I didn't have proper winter clothing and my hands turned red and hurt from the cold, but I stayed on the move through the woods. It felt warmer if I kept moving. Most of the snow had melted with a couple of warm days, but it was still cold and gray and miserable as I wandered for miles along the river without a proper coat or gloves.

I still practiced some with my knife throwing, but as long as I wasn't distracted, I was hitting the mark every time. The practice now was more to keep the edge I had with it and maybe even to score a meal, like I had when I pinned the rabbit to the log.

I was digging around in the shed one day, going through Jeremiah's tools, and sneaking a piece of deer jerky, truth be told, when I came across another tall tin can like the one on the shelf in our kitchen. There was no light in that shed and I had never seen what was underneath the shelf. When I pried the lid off, I was delighted to see more flour. Not a full can, but anything was helpful. I pulled down one of the long strips of jerky where they hung from the rafters and, carrying the jerky and the tin of flour, I went inside. Kate began shaking her head at me when she saw the meat, but she brightened considerably when I showed her the flour.

"But we ate yesterday," she said as she eyed the meat hungrily.

"Yeah, and now we eat today," I told her firmly. "You make us two small biscuits while I make some jerky soup."

"Okay John, you talked me into it." She licked her lips as she said it and I knew her mouth was watering, the same as mine. I put a pot of water over the fire and cut the deer jerky into small pieces, watching hungrily as each piece dropped in. We had put a meal together in a short time and sat down at the small table to share it. I can't say that deer jerky soup is a delicious meal, but at least the hunger pains had eased up for a while. And Kate's hot biscuit straight from the pan was absolutely fabulous.

I spent the rest of the afternoon fishing, feeling much better after even that small meal, but still to no avail. There was a layer of ice along the sides of the river and snow still on the ground in the shade. I didn't accomplish anything more than freezing my ass off out there all afternoon.

Our meals consisted of jerky soup and biscuits as long as the flour held out, which wasn't more than a week. After that, we were down to just my jerky soup, and watching as it dwindled away. It was almost the end of February now; I knew warmer springtime temperatures were just around the corner, but we still had to get by until then.

Finally, before we ran out of jerky too, I suggested to Kate that we make our way toward the Willamette. "Maybe the hunting will be better if we head west and we might have more luck fishing the Columbia."

"Perhaps," she answered thoughtfully, staring around at the cabin as if she hated to leave it.

"I don't want to leave this place either," I said as I took her chin in my hand and turned her face up to look at me. "But we don't want to sit here and starve to death."

"No…Okay. I'll begin packing."

"First thing tomorrow, then?"

"Yes, John Baker. First thing." She seemed to go right back to her happy-go-lucky self as she went about the cabin, gathering what we would need for the journey, humming a tune to herself.

CHAPTER 29

It wasn't exactly first thing when we got started on our way, Kate kept looking around the cabin, sure that we'd forgotten some impcrtant item and I was waiting for the sun to get high enough in the sky to warm things up a little. It was almost March, but still wet and chilly and windy.

Kate was excited to be going back to the Oregon Trail and she was looking forward to seeing the Willamette valley, her 'Garden of Eden.'

We stood together, her small hand in mine as we looked back at the small cabin that had given us shelter and good times. I remembered, as we stood there, how I had laughed with her and enjoyed myself more than ever in my life. We had loved and laughed and danced together in this small space, cut off from the rest of the world out here in the wilderness. It had been a sanctuary, a secluded refuge, a hideout from the rest of the world. It was hard to think about leaving and rejoining society. I knew neither of us wanted to. If we only had proper food supplies, we could stay here forever. Together. Safe and happy and warm in our love.

"Thank you, little cabin," I said, "for the good times."

Kate squeezed my hand and, as we turned to leave, we heard a lone wolf howl, far off across the hills.

We carried the deer jerky with us and we chewed on small pieces as we walked. It kept the hunger pains at bay enough to make it manageable. We walked quietly for the most part, keeping an eye out for any game we might scare up. We didn't see any our first day out and we made more of our jerky soup when we camped for the night. It was still cold and the ground was wet. We huddled together in our blankets that first night, only moving to throw more wood on our fire.

By daylight, I was missing our snug little cabin with the warm fireplace and soft down bed. I was stiff and cold and wet and miserable when I crawled out of the blankets to build up the fire. I sat there unhappily, watching the small flame grow at a creeping pace, one orange tendril licking at the wet wood, while my hands turned red and stiff from the cold. Finally, the flames crawled a little higher and I could feel a bit of heat from them.

"Maybe we shouldn't have left yet," Kate mumbled from the blankets, covering her head with them as she shivered.

"Freeze or starve, I don't like either choice," I answered in a grumpy tone.

We warmed up and dried out as the sun came up and my fire grew higher. Kate kept the blankets wrapped around her as she sat by the fire. I heated her a cup of hot water over the fire and she sipped it as she sat there. Then I shaved more of the jerky into the water heating on the fire and we enjoyed a lovely buffet of mostly hot water.

"It will be warmer in the Willamette," I told her as we stared into the flames. "We've just got to keep moving."

We got on our way again and came onto the mouth of the river where it joined with the Columbia. It was a truly amazing sight, looking out over such a great river. The brown hills were so tall here, the Columbia passed through a bit of a canyon between them. The water was a sparkling blue as the early spring sun shone onto it.

We took a noon break and I tried out my fish net, which I had taken off the frame for traveling. It didn't work as well, but after a couple hours, I did catch a trout and Kate built up the fire while I cleaned and gutted it. It made more of a meal than we had had lately and our spirits were much higher the rest of the day.

Our moccasins made walking much more comfortable; the soles had hardened enough til we didn't feel the rocks through the bottoms. Yet, it was still hard going. Even though I was leaner and tougher now, walking for miles and miles on very little food will sure take it out of you.

We had no more luck with fishing or hunting and we were resigned to our evening meal of very little jerky and plenty of hot water. I didn't say anything to Kate, but I was still pretty worried about finding enough food to get us as far as the Willamette. I knew we needed to eat more food to walk all day on the trail or we would quickly become too weak to keep going. Kate, as always, seemed completely unconcerned. "The lord will provide," was always her answer.

We made more of our jerky soup as we sat by the fire the following morning. I was really only shaving off enough pieces of jerky to flavor our soup. It wasn't anything that could really be considered a meal. It had rained some overnight and everything we had was wet. Even the wood was wet and each piece hissed when I threw it on the fire. The wet wood made enough smoke to signal a rescue plane, had there been such a thing. We sat there, cold and wet and hungry, choking on the smoke from our fire, but the need to warm up and dry out overcoming our need to move further away from the thick, white smoke.

"I sure miss that little cabin," I grumbled as I added more wet, hissing wood to the fire.

"I do too, John. But I'm sure we will make it through just fine. And then we'll build our own cabin." That brightened my mood. I pictured it as I sat there, white smoke from the fire drifting up around my face. Our own little cabin in a green, green valley. Horses and cattle grazing across the green hills. Maybe we could even get ourselves a nice dog. And a milk cow. How wonderful a big tall glass of cold milk would have tasted right now. I could see our future together as we sat there. Working and loving together on our own place. "Yeah, it'll be good in the Willamette. We'll make our own Garden of Eden," I told her.

CHAPTER 30

Kate watched the smoke drifting around John's face as he huddled over the fire. She was cold and wet and miserable too. Sleeping on the cold ground had started a cough and her lungs felt painful when she took a deep breath. She had never been one to complain; she mentioned none of it to John, but she was a little worried too. She felt sure they would be fine if they could just make it to the warmer valley, but a strange sense of foreboding was hanging like a cloud over her again. Much as it had at the mission. She couldn't put her finger on anything solid, it was just a feeling that passed over her from time to time. She shook it off as she watched John; she knew he was picturing their future together as he sat there. That's what she should be doing too, instead of being such a worrywart. She tried picturing the green valley and their own cabin as John had described it, but she hadn't seen the valley before, as he had. Try as she might, she couldn't really see it in her mind.

We didn't see any game that day and we had no luck with fishing. We probably made fifteen or twenty miles and we were too exhausted when we camped for the night to care about our empty stomachs. We chewed on a bit of the cold jerky and huddled together in our blankets. Just a few more days, I kept telling myself.

Kate was uncharacteristically quiet and I wrapped the blankets around both of us as we huddled in front of the fire.

"We *will* make it," I told her. "I know it's tough right now, but we're going to be okay."

"I know, John Baker." She turned her face up to me and gave me a smile. It lit up her face and brightened my day, but it almost seemed to me that the smile hadn't quite reached her eyes.

I dreamed of Kate as we slept on the cold, hard ground. I was chasing her through the Columbia Gorge. We were underneath the trees and running between the huge green ferns. She was laughing and spinning as she ran ahead of me. The sun was shining through the tall trees and it dappled the ground here and there. Kate seemed brighter to me with each patch of sunlight she passed through, then her coloring washed out as she reached the darkness under the trees. She was happy and laughing as she looked back at me. She ran on and on, laughing and twirling through the forest, getting deeper and deeper into their shade, until the darkness of the forest swallowed her and she disappeared.

I sat up with a start. It was pitch black and cold; the fire had died and the stars were shining brilliantly against the black sky. I put my hand up to my face. I was sweating, even though it was so cold out there. Kate rolled over on the hard ground, grumbling and pulling at the blankets. I had pulled the blankets off her when I sat up. I lay down again, pulling the blankets back over her, my mind filled with the strange dream.

We got on our way early the following morning, preferring the hard walk to sitting around on the cold ground. And at least when we were moving, it got the blood flowing and kept us warmer. Kate coughed occasionally, covering her mouth and turning her head, as if she didn't want me to hear.

"You alright?" I asked her each time she coughed.

"I'm fine, John," she insisted. "It's just from sleeping on the cold ground."

"You better not get sick again." I unrolled one of our blankets and wrapped it around her shoulders as she walked.

"Really, I'm fine John. And I'm warm enough." She started to pull the blanket off, but I wouldn't let her.

"That's what you said the last time, too." I wrapped it back around her.

The sky was overcast and heavy. Not even a morning sun to warm us as we kept moving, my free arm around her shoulders to provide a little more body heat. It was a hard walk along the river; we were hunting as we walked and following the river instead of the trail. It was either deep sand or mud and every step seemed to be harder than the one before. We still didn't scare up any game and, after a couple hours, we moved back up to the Oregon road, where wagons had worn a better trail.

A chilly spring wind came with the afternoon. The day had only warmed slightly by then, but whatever comfort we'd enjoyed quickly diminished as the wind wicked away our body heat. We had no luck with scaring up any game either. We had no choice but to camp early and find any shelter we could from the wind. We built a small fire underneath the trees and heated more of our jerky soup, then turned in early, snuggling together in the blankets. I wrapped both arms tight around Kate and pulled her warm body into my chest. "As hungry and miserable as I am out here with you," I whispered to her, "I still wouldn't trade it for my old life."

Kate kissed the hand of the arm I had wrapped around her. Her head rested on my other arm and, I wasn't sure, but I thought I felt a tear run slowly across my forearm.

We woke up to a bright morning sun peeking through the clouds. While the air was still frosty, I felt sure we would have a warmer day as the sun climbed higher. We set off with higher spirits after a small breakfast of mostly hot water.

"Today is going to be our day," I said emphatically. "It's going to be a beautiful day and we're going to find some game."

"I certainly hope you're right, John Baker. Our jerky is never going to hold out at this rate, to make it all the way to the Willamette." Kate sounded better today; she was coughing less and her eyes were brighter.

"Yeah, I know." My stomach grumbled angrily as she reminded me of how little we had eaten. We had to be looking like a couple of dirty, ragged, starved orphan children.

We did scare up a rabbit about midmorning. The rabbit surprised us as it popped out from underneath a bush several yards ahead of us. I was walking with the Bowie knife in my hand and I brought it up and threw it in one swift motion. But the rabbit had took off so quick and it zig-zagged back and forth as it ran, causing my blade to whiz right by. The rabbit was out of sight in a second and I heaved a sigh as I retrieved the knife. I felt even hungrier after having come so close to having a meal. We saw no more game that day and we were resigned to shaving off a little more of our jerky into a pot of water for dinner. I even tried fishing while Kate set up our camp, but I had no luck there either. We had been so many days without a proper meal, indeed, so many weeks now without a proper meal, I felt as if my body—which had been feeling so strong and fit—was weakening without proper nutrition.

We hunted as we walked the next day. We had skipped a morning meal in hopes that we could catch some early morning game on the move. We still saw nothing and I'd had no more luck with the fishing, but I knew we had to be coming close to the Indian village again and I was willing to beg, barter or steal a meal. We still had some of our jerky, but it wasn't going to last long at this rate.

We were walking along the ridge of a small brown hill, looking over the beauty of the Columbia, when I saw a movement in the water.

"What is that?" Kate asked.

I didn't answer as I saw it disappear, then pop back up. I dropped the pack off my back and took off down the hill at a dead run. I kept my eye on the dark spot in the water as it disappeared, then resurfaced a little further down, the current pulling it away from me.

It was a young Indian boy, probably seven or eight years old, and he disappeared under the water again as I reached the edge of the river. I jumped in, clothes and all, and saw him resurface a little further down, coughing and sputtering. The current was pulling him downriver away from me. I swam through the icy water as hard as I could, grabbing him around his chest. He immediately pulled my head under the water in his panic and I felt the strength seeping from my arms and legs from the near-freezing water. I held him out at arms-length and made my slow way back to the bank, barely keeping his head and my own above the surface as I paddled one-handed. The cold sapped my strength even faster than the struggling child. Each stroke I swam toward the shore was harder than the one before. Meanwhile, the current pulled us both further downstream, away from Kate.

Kate ran downriver, carrying both our packs, and met us at the bank. She reached for the boy's arm and pulled him onto the bank, where he lay, shivering and exhausted. I crawled out of the water, literally crawled on my hands and knees, my body gone weak and numb from the cold. I felt so weak, I thought she was going to have to pull me in too. I dropped down onto my stomach on the bank and waited for my heartbeat to slow and some strength to return to my arms and legs. I think I was beyond shivering; I felt only numb and weak as I lay there panting. Kate raced around, gathering wood for a fire. I crawled to it as the flames curled higher, dragging the small boy with me. He hadn't moved from where she had put him on the bank. He lay there gasping for breath, his little chest heaving.

I pulled him in front of me by the fire while Kate pulled our blankets out, wrapping them around both of us. We sat and shivered for a while, but slowly dried out as Kate continually fed the fire. I could feel my strength slowly returning as the heat seeped through my wet clothing.

Kate heated hot water and we sipped it as we sat there. I could see color returning to the boy's face as he warmed up. As he grew warmer and began to dry out, the boy chattered at us in his language. There wasn't one word we understood, but we nodded along while he chattered.

"He must be from the village nearby," Kate offered.

"I guess. When we're completely dry, I guess we can take him there and see."

The kid bounced back quicker than me, he was on his feet once he was dry and waving at us to follow him.

"Okay, okay little dude," I told him as he beckoned.

We put the fire out and followed him on down the trail, where he did indeed lead us to the village. It was the same one where Kate lost her horse to the mountain lion and we had traded off the wagon. I think some of those men might have recognized us when they came out of their lodges. That little dude raised such a ruckus, he roused the whole village. I saw one man making straight for me, a stern look on his face as the little boy chattered. The man moved so fast toward me and had such a look on his face, I was contemplating pulling the Bowie from my leg. I hadn't forgot about all those people getting killed at the mission. But when he grabbed my forearm and clapped me on the back with his free hand, I knew the boy must be telling him how I had saved him from the river.

"Thaa..nk yo..u," the man said slowly, drawing the words out as if he wasn't used to using them. "Come, eat." He motioned putting food in his mouth and we followed him to his fire, where the boy was already surrounded by the women of the village, getting hugs all around as he chattered.

"How do you shut this kid up?" I whispered to Kate. She only smiled, amused by the whole ordeal. I think those people were regarding me as a hero. They dished up bowls of food for both of us as we sat by their fire and the men brought chunks of deer from a small pit near the lodge. They had been roasting the whole deer on coals in that pit and it was the most tender, delicious meat I'd ever had in my life. Of course, when you're starving, I guess anything would've tasted wonderful. I'm not sure what was in the bowl, some kind of stew I think, but it was wonderful too. Whatever it was, it had vegetables in it, something we had been in need of for a while. I could feel my strength returning as I ate the hot food.

Everyone in the village began pulling roasted chunks of meat off the deer and it turned into somewhat of a party. The Indians ate, then smoked long pipes as a few people began dancing. Some of the older ones sang and chanted as the young ones danced and stomped their feet, while the children ran around the circle of people, laughing and playing. I caught their excitement as I watched them enjoying themselves. I pulled Kate up from the ground and we joined in the dancing, doing some of the moves I'd taught her. Those Indians stopped dancing and watched us; they seemed completely amazed by the moves. They laughed and pointed until a few of them even tried the moves themselves.

We had ourselves a wonderful time until late into the night, then the same big Indian came to us and pointed toward one of the lodges. "Sleep," he told us. I bowed my head at him and we went inside. It was a crude building, but warm and comfortable and we were happy to be indoors for the night. It felt like a year since we had slept inside, dry and warm, our appetites happily sated. We had really eaten very little. Our stomachs had shrank from near-starvation until we could really hold very little.

CHAPTER 31

Kate had enjoyed her day immensely. From watching John rescue the young boy in the morning, to dancing with him around the fire in the evening. He never ceased to amaze her as she watched him leap into the river and rescue the boy and accept the Indian man's thanks with an embarrassed nod. John had jumped into action without hesitation from the time they met. From saving the two of them from bandits, to sitting with her in the river to break her fever, she couldn't have dreamed up a better man to spend the rest of her life with. And, spending the evening with these kind and interesting Indians had been a fun experience too. After months of holing up in the cabin alone together, dancing with a group of people had been wonderful. She had seen so much love and laughter in the eyes of the Indians, she would almost be sorry to leave them. Kate smiled in the dark and sighed heavily as she snuggled closer into John's chest and felt his arm tighten around her.

We were on our way just after sunup the following morning, after the same big Indian took my forearm in what I guessed was a handshake and bowed his head to me.

Several people from the village came out and waved and one of the women brought a haunch of venison and bowed her head as she handed it to Kate.

"Thank you," Kate said as she bowed her head in return.

We made our way back up to the trail and the little boy I'd saved came running up the hill, waving and chattering at us as he kept pace alongside us. It had been an interesting adventure, and one I knew I would never forget. To have made a village full of friends in this wilderness was not something either of us had counted on. I was a little confused as I thought about it. How was it possible that the Indians had massacred those folks at the mission, when the ones we'd run across had been so helpful and kind?

We'd soon left the village behind and the day was slowly warming as the sun peeked through the clouds.

"Look there," I said to Kate. There were a hundred or more fat Indian ponies grazing across the hills on the north side of the river. "It's called Horse Heaven Hills in the future," I told her. "I guess now I understand why."

"They're beautiful," she said quietly. "I wish we had a few of them."

"Or even one. A pack horse would be helpful."

"Poor Nip. I hope he found a good home."

"I'm sure he did. Maybe the men at the fort took him in."

We stopped for our noon break on a rise overlooking the Columbia. I got a fire going and then shaved the bark off a couple sticks with the Bowie knife.

We impaled chunks of venison on the sticks and held them over the fire, keeping them slowly turning. We had enough of the deer to get through at least a couple days if we were careful.

After lunch, Kate took her mother's jewelry box from her pack and opened it, showing me the contents. She pulled out a string of pearls and held them up. "I think I can use these to trade for seeds and a plow to start our farm," she said thoughtfully.

"No Kate, I don't want you to let go of your mother's jewelry."

"I don't think she'd mind, John. She would be happy that we were finishing the journey that she and my father began. And we're going to need something to get us started."

"Maybe I should take on some sort of job for a while." I scratched the stubble on my face as I thought about it. "We're going to need plow horses and furniture and a barn. We've really got our work cut out for us, little one."

"I know, John Baker, but we can handle anything." She jumped into my lap and wrapped her arms around my neck.

I buried my face into her neck as I held her tight, breathing in her sweet scent. "Yeah, we can handle it," I told her. "As long as we're together, we can do anything."

I described the Columbia River Gorge to her as we walked. "You'll see it soon," I told her. "The fir trees are so tall and it stays so wet and rainy through there, even the things that should be brown are green. Even the trunks of the trees are green with moss. There's literally moss growing on every surface."

"It sounds beautiful," she said excitedly. "We saw so much brown and barren crossing the Great American Desert. I can't wait to see it."

"There's also a waterfall that's over six hundred feet high. And there are huge rocky cliffs that hang out over the water."

"Oh, it sounds amazing, John Baker."

"I've always been amazed by it. It seems almost mystical when you go through there. Like something out of a fantasy movie. No matter how many times I've passed through it, I've never grown tired of the drive."

She took my hand as she bounced around me happily. "Tell me about the Pacific ocean."

"Just imagine, as far as the eye can see, nothing but beautiful blue water, dropping right off the edge of the horizon. And the waves come onshore and crash against huge boulders, sending spray into the air. There's always a wind off the ocean out there and so much salt in the air, you can taste it."

Kate stopped, closing her eyes and tilting her head back as she pictured it in her mind. Never being one to waste an opportunity, I moved in closer and, slipping my hand under her hair and onto her neck, I brought my lips down to hers while her eyes were still closed. She responded instantly, as we stood there in the wilderness, making out like a couple of teenagers.

We had some of the deer for dinner and curled up by the fire after, her head on my chest. We made plans for our future together and, although I missed my family horribly, I was looking forward to spending my life here with my true love. "Maybe I should get a job for a while. Maybe something like a lumber mill. We are going to need money to make this dream come true. And I don't want you selling off your mother's jewelry," I said firmly.

"Whatever you think is best, John Baker."

"No." I sat up, forcing her to sit up too and look at me. "I know that's the way things were done here, but it's not my way."

"What do you mean, John?"

"I mean, we make all our decisions together. Equal partners. Okay?"

"Okay, John. I like your future ways." She smiled up at me—her blue, blue eyes sparkling at me—until I leaned down and kissed her passionately.

The temperature had been pretty decent all day, with a warm sun beating on our backs as we walked, but it dipped overnight and we huddled together in our blankets, sharing body heat.

CHAPTER 32

I dreamed of the lone wolf again that night. It was chasing a guy with white hair through the river, but then, as dreams are known for doing, the river turned into the Pacific Ocean and the wolf chased the white haired man right off the edge of the horizon.

I remembered the dream when I first woke up the following morning, when I was still half awake and hadn't yet opened my eyes. It was weird and distorted and I didn't know who the man was. Once I opened my eyes and sat up, the dream was gone and I sat there for a minute, trying to recall it.

We made ourselves a hot jerky soup for breakfast, saving the rest of the deer for our dinner. I knew we would need it after a full days walk. The wind off the river was strong all day and we moved uphill into the trees where it wasn't as bad.

"We're getting near the gorge now," I explained as we walked. "The winds can be pretty fierce coming upriver. Sometimes, they're so strong, it makes the river look like its moving in the opposite direction."

"Walking into a headwind feels like we're wading through water," Kate said as she huffed and puffed.

We finished off the deer and spent another chilly night huddled together. We had found a valley between two hills where we could make a fire and have a little shelter from the unceasing winds. Moving uphill away from the river had meant an even harder walk for us all day. It was up one hill, then back down and immediately up the next. We were both cold and exhausted and the Willamette valley was beginning to sound like Eden to me too.

We made a little more jerky soup for breakfast, but it was really plenty of hot water and very little jerky. We still had a couple hundred miles to go and not a lot of our precious jerky left.

The wind had let up some as we walked, but we stuck to the hills in the morning, watching for game. We were quiet as we walked and we moved slower as we kept our eyes peeled for any movement, but unfortunately, the only thing we saw was a coyote, slinking across the hill ahead of us. He looked back at us as he trotted, then quickly disappeared over the hill. I carried the Bowie in my hand, ready to throw it at the first rabbit I saw. Kate walked with the musket at the ready, but after a few miles her arms grew tired and she slung it back over her shoulder.

We finally gave it up by afternoon and tried our hand at fishing. It was a little more difficult with our net in the bigger, wider river, but we kept at it and Kate squealed in surprise when I came up out of the water with a decent size steelhead. Our stomachs were grumbling with hunger and Kate quickly built a fire as I cleaned the fish.

"It's delicious," Kate said as we stuffed ourselves on the pink meat.

"Wonderful," I agreed.

We only finished off half the fish and we wrapped up the other half for later, then set out, our stomachs happily sated.

We were getting closer to the gorge now. There were tall cliffs on our left as we walked. We either had to walk up and down hills or stay closer to the riverbank, but even then, we often sunk into deep mud.

We made our camp down near the river. We found a spot between two logs where the ground was relatively dry. We built a small fire between them and made our bed behind it. I leaned back onto our packs and looked at the stars and the moon. It was a full moon and, as it rose, the silvery light played off the river. It even cast a silver tint to the grasses across the hills.

Kate came and sat down beside me and curled up into my chest.

"If I were home right now, I probably would have been inside, watching TV, and I would have missed all this, the way the moon plays off the water and how it turns the trees and grasses silver."

"Yes, but you would be warm and dry and well-fed."

"Okay, good point. But it wouldn't matter if you weren't there with me."

"I feel the same, John Baker. I thank God every day for sending you back through time to be with me."

I leaned forward and kissed the top of her head, feeling damn lucky to be alive. God had certainly taught me a lesson too. It seemed silly now to think that only a few short months ago, I had thought my life was over and I wanted to die. I would have missed out on the best time of my life, not to mention the fact that now I had finally learned the meaning of real love, not just the physical attraction, not just the chemistry between two people, but the kind of love you see between two elderly folk who've already passed their fiftieth wedding anniversary. We had become the best of friends and partners, and I knew that Kate was that one person I wanted to spend the rest of my life with, that one special person I would be willing to die for.

We walked hand in hand along the river the next morning, enjoying the peacefulness of this place, the sound of the water and the breeze through the trees. I thanked God again, as I walked, for sending me back through time to spend the rest of my life with this amazing woman and for showing me just how much I had to live for.

We took our noon break alongside the river, cooking the remainder of the fish we'd caught. It wasn't much, but fortunately, we didn't require much.

"We should stop a little earlier today," I told Kate. "Hopefully we can catch another fish and have a nice dinner."

"Really? Two meals in one day? I don't think I could hold that much food, John."

"Okay, who taught you to be such a smartass?"

Kate only gave me a knowing smile, blue eyes sparkling with mischief, and I pulled her close for a kiss.

We did stop earlier as planned and I did catch a small trout as planned. Even though it was small, it was plenty for us. Our stomachs had shrunk to the point, I thought maybe Kate was right. Who needs to eat two meals every day? We were thrilled to have even one.

We reached a small village the following day, it wasn't even a village really, just a few houses and buildings overlooking the river. It looked more like a white man's village with log cabins and outhouses, but I didn't trust any strangers, after what we'd already seen in this harsh land. We didn't see any people moving around it, but we skirted the village anyway by climbing through the hills behind it. The Columbia looked even more beautiful from up high in the hills, although it looked so different from my own time, it was hard to get my bearings.

Late in the afternoon, we came upon an Indian village where the river looked so different than how I remembered it, I would've swore it wasn't the Columbia. The river was narrow here and picking up speed as it made its way between huge black rocks. It turned to whitewater as it plunged through and a little further down, there was a good-sized waterfall with what I guessed was a fifteen or twenty foot drop.

"None of this is here in my time," I told Kate.

"That's silly, John. Where could it go?"

"There's a huge dam right about here somewhere," I said pointing downriver. "It's called The Dalles Dam. I guess it flooded all this area when they built it. Plus there's two other dams back up the river from here. That's why none of this looks the same to me now. I never realized this river was so narrow and shallow in the past." Kate stared at the river, trying to imagine it as I described it in my own time. We were still up in the hills, looking down on the amazing views. As we looked down on the falls and the rushing whitewater, a bald eagle came downriver, soaring right over our heads. It was so close above us, I could see one eye when it cocked its head to look at us. What a huge, beautiful bird in this amazing time and place. I had only ever seen a couple of bald eagles in my life and certainly not from so close. Before, it had been from a vehicle window and off in the distance. Truly, this entire area I had never seen as I did now. Not just the fact of being in a different time, no, it was the fact of walking it and living it, instead of just driving past it.

There were Indians standing in the water below us and more were standing on the bank, fishing. They looked small from where we stood on the hillside. I knew how cold that water was, even in the summertime, it never warmed up. It was fed from melting glaciers. Yet these men stood in it in the chilly spring weather as if it were bath water.

We skirted on around them too, staying up high in the hills, and went back to hunting as we walked.

CHAPTER 33

The temperatures had improved once we were in the gorge. I knew the winds could still be ferocious, but we'd had a couple of balmy days and the temperature dropped only a little at night.

"It'll be getting warmer and wetter as we continue west. There's a good chance we'll be sleeping on some pretty soggy ground the rest of the way."

"That's fine, John. I'm looking forward to getting there and building our own house. I want a garden and flowers and big trees. Are there large trees there?"

"Huge trees. Conifers and Oregon pine and Pacific Firs. They're some of the biggest trees in the country."

"How far do we still have to go?"

"Only another hundred miles or so. Should be nothing for you, after walking all the way from Missouri."

"I can handle it."

We moved back down toward the river, thinking maybe we could catch a fish for our dinner. As we pushed through the weeds and came out onto the sandy bank, a huge white bird took flight over the river. It must have been standing in the water's edge as we'd come down the hill. I lifted the musket and fired off a shot, leading it a little with the rifle as it took flight. The gun boomed and the bird dropped, right into the cold, swift current. I dropped the pack off my back and took off after it, splashing into the freezing water. The current was pulling the bird away from me and I had to swim hard to catch it. It felt like the icy water was sucking the very life from my muscles. I could feel my arms and legs weakening, but starvation made me determined. I grabbed the dead bird by the neck and swam straight into the bank, then made my way back upriver, where Kate stood, shading her eyes with her hand as she watched me. I held the bird up by its neck as I let out a whoop. "Dinner is served, my lady."

"I think that's a crane, John. I don't think I've ever eaten a water bird like that before."

"You've had duck and goose, haven't you?"

"Yes."

"Same thing, just a little bigger."

She started a fire while I stripped off my wet clothes, hanging them over bushes to dry. I quickly pulled on the other set of clothing, but I was still shivering from head to toe, until the flames finally blazed up into a decent size fire.

"You know, back in 2010, I certainly never took a freezing bath, washed my clothes, and swam to catch dinner at the same time."

Kate threw her head back and laughed, a happy, lilting sound ringing out across the silence of our wilderness. "You are silly, John Baker," she said. "But you sure do make me laugh."

"Yeah…well, you know it's the best medicine."

"The best for what?"

"For everything. Laughter cures everything."

"Great. I'll remember that next time I get the measles."

Now it was my turn to laugh at her. Just knowing that we had a meal in front of us had lightened our mood and made our evening a joyous occasion. We dined well on the huge bird and wrapped up the remainder for later. The crane tasted much like duck, but with more of a wild game flavor. I leaned back onto a fallen log after stuffing myself, feeling sated and proud of myself. Kate came and sat beside me and I pulled her into my shoulder, my arm tight around her small waist.

"One thing I've learned for sure out here in the wilderness, little one."

"What's that, John?"

"Never, ever take a meal for granted, cause you don't know where the next one's coming from."

She giggled against my chest. "You got that right, John Baker. At least once we're established in the Willamette, we can have chickens and cows and a garden. It won't always be this hard."

"I know, little one." I brought my other arm around her too as I held her small body, my heart filled with such a deep love for her. It was getting hard to remember what my life had been like before her. It was as if she had filled a hole in my heart or as if I was never a whole person until I met her and now, I was complete.

"What do you miss most from your world?" She asked quietly. "Other than your family, I mean."

I was quiet too as I considered it. I thought about all the electronics, phones, TV's and computers; things that a few months ago I thought I couldn't live without. And now, not even an electrical outlet. But no, I hadn't even thought about all the electronics I'd left behind in months. I couldn't really say I had missed them.

"A hot shower," I said suddenly as it came to me. "I would give my left arm for a hot shower right now."

"Can you describe it for me?"

"You turn on a faucet and step into hot water, instead of heating it over the fire. It's like standing under a hot, steaming waterfall."

"Mm, sounds wonderful," she murmured into my chest. I lay down flat and pulled the blankets over us when I realized that the hard walk combined with the full stomach was putting her to sleep.

"I love you, John Baker," she mumbled.

"I love you too, little one."

CHAPTER 34

We had veered off the path, wandering through the undergrowth in search of small game. I had the Bowie knife in my hand and the small one in the scabbard tucked into the top edge of my moccasin. Kate was walking quietly behind me, watching where she put each foot to make as little noise as possible.

We still had some of the bird left and I was hoping for another huge, happy dinner like the night before.

All of a sudden, I heard a dull thud, like a *whoomp,* and I heard Kate grunt behind me. It felt like slow motion as I turned and looked into those beautiful ice-blue eyes. Her eyes were wide with confusion and terror as she slowly fell toward me. I felt frozen in shock and confusion as I watched her falling toward me. She hit the ground on her stomach before I could even move and I saw an Indian tomahawk buried in her back. An ice-cold steel gripped my heart and spread through my body as I looked at her. I could see blood pooling around her as my legs turned to rubber and I dropped to my knees beside her, my mind going numb. I heard a *thwack* just as I dropped down. A knife had been thrown and was sticking out of a tree behind me. Had I not dropped down at that very instant, that knife would have been sticking out of *me*. I slowly pulled the weapon from Kate's back, tossing it to the side and I watched in complete horror as the blood flowed freely. I turned her over with her head in my lap. Her blue eyes stared up into mine...imploring...beseeching. I heard a movement behind me and, turning my upper body, I brought the Bowie knife up and threw it in one swift motion, straight into the chest of a man coming toward me. I saw another knife in his hand as he dropped. He went down with a groan and I gently lay Kate's head on the ground, ran over and snatched the knife from his grasping hands. I left him where he fell and quickly returned to Kate. "I'm gonna roll you onto your side so I can stop the bleeding."

She stared up at me, her face was so pale and her eyes looked huge in her little round pixie face. I gently rolled her to her side, took my shirt off and used it to staunch the flow of blood. It quickly became drenched and I applied more pressure. She seemed to be having trouble breathing so I rolled her back over, keeping my hand and shirt over the wound. It didn't seem to be helping, though. There was just *so* much blood. I could feel it seeping through my fingers where I held her.

"I love you, John Baker. You know that, don't you?" Her voice was so weak. Nothing like my merry, happy-go-lucky Kate.

"I know you do, little one. And I love you... more than life itself."

She didn't answer and her eyes were closing.

"No Kate, stay with me." I shook her a little to keep her with me. There was no response and I could feel my heart beating wildly as a dark cloud of doom swept down over me. Her eyes were closed now and she didn't open them as I called her name. I put my fingers on her neck and felt for a pulse. I kept trying and trying, moving my fingers up and down her neck. I put both hands on her shoulders and shook her again, a little harder this time. "Come on Kate...don't you leave me."

She was gone. My beautiful Kate...my sweet little one...was gone. Right in front of my eyes, as I sat there, helpless. There was nothing I could do to stop her from leaving me. She looked as if she was sleeping peacefully on the ground, her long blond hair fanned out around her. But my heart knew what my mind refused to accept. I had traveled back through time to find the sweetest, purest love I had ever known, only to lose her to some madman with a tomahawk. Yet, my mind still rejected the idea. It could only be another of my crazy dreams. No way could it be more than a dream, a nightmare...it had to be.

My head came up as I remembered the guy with my knife in his chest. A rage came over me unlike anything I'd ever known. It was a cold, deadly, murderous rage, a white-hot fire burning through my body as I realized what this psycho had done to my sweet Kate.

I ran back through the bushes. He was dragging himself slowly through the undergrowth away from me. His chest was covered in blood and he had left a red streak across the ground. When I reached him, he half-turned to look at me and I brought my foot up and kicked him as hard as I could in the stomach. He cried out in pain and I grabbed his collar and drug him back through the undergrowth. He was kicking and flailing, but I ignored him. The white-hot fire had turned into a coldness. My brain was numb, my body moved as if of its own accord. I was completely unthinking, unfeeling as I pulled him back into the clearing. Out of the corner of my eye, I could see Kate's still form lying in the trees. My heart lurched and I felt my knees giving out again. I knew I must be in a state of shock because my mind refused to accept the fact that she was gone. I quickly looked away and turned back to our attacker.

"Why?" I asked him. I had meant to sound forceful, but my voice cracked with emotion.

"You killed my two brothers a few months ago." He was only just getting his breath back where I had kicked it out of him. "I was going to kill you too. Slow and painful-like. I been tracking you for two weeks, since I got here from Fort Boise."

"But not Kate," I choked out. "She didn't do anything."

"She was with you."

I didn't say anything else. I went to my pack and pulled out my rawhide strips, the thickest ones I had. I began tying each piece together slowly, making each knot hard and tight, while the scumbag watched. My knife was still sticking out of his chest and he held his hand around the blade, trying to stop the bleeding.

"What are you going to do?"

I didn't say anything. He had his answer when I tied a noose in one end and slipped it around his neck. He started crying and begging me for his life. I was cold all over, completely apathetic. I felt no more than that lone wolf would feel as she takes down a deer. I drug him by his neck, kicking and screaming, over to a tree with a low enough limb. I threw my end over the limb, pulled my bloody knife from his chest, wiped it on his shirt and started pulling until his feet left the ground. I held my end while he kicked and thrashed, until finally he grew still, then I tied the end of the rawhide rope I was holding through his belt and left him hanging there. I showed no mercy, in fact, I didn't feel anything as I strung him up from the tree. I only felt cold and numb throughout my body. It was as if my mind had switched off the instant Kate left me.

I stumbled back over to her, dropping on the ground beside her. I pulled her lifeless body into my arms and held her. I must have held her and cried for an hour or more. "Why, God?" I screamed at the Heavens. "Why her instead of me?" I truly did not want to live without her. I had only thought I knew what true love was before her. She was my soul mate, my destiny. It wasn't supposed to end this way, before we even had a chance to spend our lives together. And what of our farm…our Garden of Eden? I had pictured us growing old there together. I sat on the wet ground, holding her, until my legs had grown numb from the cold. I tried to think of what I could do, but my brain just wouldn't seem to work right. Couldn't I travel back in time again and stop this from happening? Was there some way I could go with her? My mind finally cleared enough as I sat there, to consider what Kate would want me to do. I remembered how saddened she had been that she hadn't been able to give her parents a decent burial. I carried her lifeless body up the hill to a spot overlooking the river. "Your parent's may not have had a decent burial, but you will," I told her as I looked at her still body, my heart breaking. No, not breaking. It wasn't a strong enough word. I felt like my heart had been torn from my chest and, if I buried her here, in this cold, wet ground, I would be burying a piece of me there with her. I wrapped her in a blanket and began to dig in the soft black dirt. I worked at it for a couple of hours, until I had a deep enough hole.

But when I looked at the still form underneath the blanket, my little remaining strength drained from my body and I sank down on the ground beside her. I just didn't think I could go through with it. I knew I wasn't thinking clearly, images of the happy times we'd shared on the trail and in the cabin danced across my eyes whenever I tried to think. I tried closing my eyes, but I only saw her more clearly, dancing away from me across the cabin floor.

"Screw it," I said after I had sat there beside her for a few minutes. I acted on impulse as I picked her up and carried her with me, back down the hill. There was a huge rock sticking out over the river. I carried her as I walked out on it and sat down, her body across my lap. There was a cold wind coming out of the west, it made the water choppy; it almost looked like the water was flowing east instead of west. I lay down on the rock beside her, exhausted and broken. I was still trying to clear my muddled thoughts as I held her hand.

I must have fell asleep, her small, cold hand still tucked in mine and, in my troubled sleep, I thought it was her fingers moving through my hair instead of the wind.

I dreamed of Kate. She spun away from me across the cabin floor, dancing and twirling, the blue dress billowing out around her as I watched. Now I saw her walking along the river, strolling slowly in the shadows of the huge trees. She moved toward me, but she blurred in my vision as I watched her. She looked like something from a movie, a camera trick causing a blur around her body. Then she began to run and, as she ran toward me, I saw the lone wolf chasing her, chasing her through my dreams. "Stop! Kate!" I tried to call out in my dream, but no sound would cross my lips. I watched as Kate ran out onto a rock with the wolf on her heels and, without stopping, she dropped right off into the river.

I woke with a start. It seemed to be late in the night. In the confused state between sleep and waking, I really thought I had just had a horrible nightmare. The truth crashed in on me brutally as I sat up and saw Kate's lifeless body there beside me. I ran my hands across my face and rubbed my eyes, wishing I could start this day over and do things differently.

Finally, I stood up, lifting Kate's body with me and, without stopping to think it through, I leaped forward out over the fast moving river. I couldn't get as far out as I had from the middle of the bridge. I felt a stick or something stab the calf of my leg when I hit the freezing water and I let go of Kate as the pain hit, wrapping both hands around my leg as my head went under. I instantly realized what I had done and when I surfaced, I reached in the dark for Kate's body, but the river had stolen it from me. The water was swift and freezing cold and I was swept along in the current, white hot pain shooting through my leg. I treaded water against the strong current as I looked around desperately for Kate, but I couldn't see anything in the darkness. I felt around with my arms, I kicked my legs, trying with all my might to reach out and touch her. "Kate!" I yelled across the undulating water, as if she were going to answer me and I'd be able to track the sound of her voice. I grew weaker as the near-freezing water sucked the strength from my arms and legs. It was getting hard to keep myself afloat, much less look for Kate as the blood leached away from my extremities. But I tried anyway; it felt as if I was moving in slow motion now as I searched for her body. I couldn't see anything in the dark, black swirling water. The current was carrying me along and now, I didn't even know where I was. My brain had already been foggy, but now it seemed to be shutting down altogether. I finally stopped flailing, letting my body relax, and I closed my eyes, feeling the current dragging me down and down, ending this painful journey I'd began up on the steel girders of the bridge. *I'm coming Kate*, was my last coherent thought.

CHAPTER 35

When I opened my eyes again, my mother was leaning over a nightstand beside me, pouring a cup of water from a pitcher. When she stood up and saw me looking at her, she squealed like she'd seen a mouse and she dropped over my chest, hugging me and crying. My two brothers came into the room sounding like a stampede of horses when they heard my mom cry out. When they saw me awake, they each hugged me and cheered and made so much noise, my mother finally sent them out of the room.

"Oh John," she said, wiping the tears from her eyes, "it's so good to see you again."

"How long was I out?" It felt like only minutes ago when I leapt off the rock.

"Since November," she said as she reached out and moved my hair out of my eyes.

"That's impossible," I said, my eyes growing wide. "I just jumped with Kate's body."

Kate! It all came back in a rush as I remembered jumping in the river and accidentally letting go of her. How could I have been so stupid? "Did you find a girl's body with me?"

"No sweetie. A couple of fishermen pulled you into their boat back in November. Was there someone else with you?"

Oh Kate. I'm sorry. I squeezed my eyes shut tight as my stomach wrenched and I felt tears squeeze out of the corners. I had planned to give her a decent burial and instead, I lost her to the river. I'm not even sure what I had been thinking, to jump into the river with her, instead of giving her the burial she would have wanted.

I heard the door closing as my mother stepped out of the room. I guess she had seen the tears squeezing from my eyes and wanted to give me some privacy. "Mom," I called out.

She opened the door and stuck her head back in, "yes son?"

"Was last night the time change?"

"Yes." She sounded surprised at my question. "Spring forward," she said lightly, then closed the door.

The pain was overwhelming as I lay there staring at the ceiling, wondering why God would take Kate and not let me go with her. And how is it possible that my mother is telling me I've been here since November? Was it possible that I had been in a coma and dreamed the last six months? I felt very confused as I lay there, but Kate was clear in my head, her beautiful blue eyes, her high-spirited attitude, her laughter ringing out in the small cabin.

I felt a pain in my right leg and reached down, running my hand across my calf. Sure enough, there was a fresh stab wound on my leg and it hurt like hell. But it didn't hurt nearly as much as the pain in my heart. It just couldn't be possible that I had lost her. Not just losing her to the river, but losing the one person I'd wanted to spend the rest of my life with. I felt the fog slipping back over my mind as I tried to deal with the pain.

My mother came back in a while, carrying a plate of food and a tall glass of soda over ice. I stared at it for a bit before I could even take a sip. It had been so long since I'd had a soda or even seen an ice cube. I ate some of the dinner, but I really didn't have much of an appetite and of course, my stomach had shrunk from weeks of near starvation.

My mother sat down in a chair beside me and watched me while I ate. When I finished, she set the plate to the side and stared at me. "Who is Kate?"

I heaved a deep breath as I looked at her, wondering if I should lie. But I knew my mother, she would see right through me, just like when I was a kid.

"I jumped off that bridge and landed in 1847. I met Kate on the Oregon Trail and then lived with her in a cabin on the Walla Walla all winter."

"John. You fell off a bridge in November and you've been in a coma," she said sternly. Her voice softened and she brushed the shaggy hair off my forehead. "You only dreamed it, sweetie, you've been right here with us. Until yesterday, you had tubes and wires and machines hooked to you."

I started shaking my head back and forth on the pillow. I could hear Kate's lilting, musical voice over the sound of the rattling wagons on the trail. I remembered all too well how my legs had grown numb while I sat with her unconscious body in the river.

"Wait, what happened yesterday?"

"You sat up suddenly in bed and yelled something, I'm not sure what. The nurse said it was unintelligible. She said you were only sleeping after that instead of comatose."

I shook my head some more, disbelieving. "I learned to throw knives and hunted with them." I picked the steak knife up off my plate as I said it and flipped it in my hand, holding it by the blade. I watched my mother's eyes grow wide in horror as I flung it across the room and heard it *thwack* into the drywall.

"I could never do that before," I said coldly.

"But it had to be a dream, John. You've been right here. You hit your head when you fell in the river. You had a huge bump and a cut on the side of your head when they brought you home. Your mind must be playing tricks on you."

My head did feel fuzzy and I was so confused. *Had I dreamed it?* No, damn it, I remember Kate had torn up a sheet and wrapped it around my head. I reached up, rubbing the small scar under my hair. I remembered how much my head hurt and how silly I must have looked, with a piece of Kate's sheet wrapped around my head. "There's no way I dreamed the last six months with her, laughing and loving and dancing together."

"Oh, John," now she had tears in her eyes, "you always were such a romantic."

She picked up my dinner plate and left then, saying I needed to rest. She stopped on her way and pulled the knife from the drywall, working it up and down to free it.

"It happened, mom," I said quietly.

She gave me one last worried look over her shoulder and left.

Brad and Jake came in after a few minutes, both of them looking worried too. She must have told them my crazy-sounding story. They both looked uncomfortable as they approached.

"It's okay," I said, "I'm not going to bite you."

"Guess we're a little more worried about you throwing knives at us," Brad said with a smile.

"Do you guys think I'm crazy?"

"Well," Jake said playfully, "you always were a little crazy."

"The human brain is still a mystery," Brad said uncomfortably.

"Yeah, that was a pretty damn real dream, though."

"But you were in a coma," Brad said in a serious tone. "I read that when people are comatose, they experience some pretty crazy things. Some have said they've even been to Heaven and back."

"Hey," Jake chimed in. "I saw that on a show once. This lady was in a coma and she said she saw Heaven and her dead grandmother while she was asleep."

"Yeah, that must be it," I agreed, figuring it was the easiest way to get this over with. And, oddly enough, Kate *was* beginning to look like a dream when I pictured her in my mind. I rubbed the scar on my head absentmindedly as I thought about it. My mind had been in such a fog and now, it felt like the fog was closing in around all conscious thought. I was completely torn between the pain in my heart and the logic of what everyone was telling me.

They both gave me a hug and said how glad they were that I was back from my coma, then they left, heading for their own homes and families.

I lay there for hours, thinking about Kate. How could anything that real have been a dream? And the love I felt for her, it was too real. I felt broken inside, as if my heart had been ripped from my chest when I lost her. I could see the pale blue dress floating around her as we both fell toward the river. *Had I dreamed that?* My head felt cloudy and the longer I thought about it, the more unsure I became.

I finally drifted into a fitful sleep, filled with dreams of Kate, dancing and twirling in front of me one minute with her blue eyes sparkling, falling in slow motion toward the water the next, the blue dress floating around her like a cloud.

I was half awake with the first rays of sun peeking through the curtains when my mom came in, carrying a tray filled with sausage, eggs, toast and fruit. My stomach churned as I looked at so much food. *How had I ever eaten so much in one meal?* It seemed a lifetime ago since I had leaped off that bridge.

My mother sat down beside me and watched me pick at the food. She talked about my brothers and the farm, filling me in on the last six months. I nodded occasionally, feigning interest when all I could really think about was Kate.

She gave up finally and left me alone with my thoughts. My mind was still a confused fog, caught between memories of Kate and the logical explanation of a comatose dream. I crawled out of bed and onto my feet. My leg hurt like hell and another near-death experience had left me a little dizzy, or maybe it was the fact of spending six months in bed? My mind still refused to accept that fact, no matter how hard I tried to believe it. I made my way slowly to the bathroom and turned on the shower. I stood under it for damn near a half hour, letting the steaming hot water wash over me. The luxurious smell of the soap and shampoo, the feel of the hot spray across my shoulders, it was an experience that I'd thought I would never know again and I reveled in it. I thought about our cabin as I stood there and how long it took to heat water on the fire, and of sitting in the small tub to bathe. It almost seemed like a culture shock to turn on a faucet and have hot water. Had I really had such an elaborate dream?

I stayed at the farm with my mother for a few days, and Brad and Jake stopped by every day to visit, but truthfully, I was a changed man. Or more accurately, I had left a boy and came back a man. I studied my body in a full-length mirror. I was a little underweight now, but still broad and muscled. Every inch of my body was lean, solid muscle after my months of hard labor. How was it possible that I was lying in a bed here with my body wasting away, while I was there getting stronger and leaner? My muscles should have atrophied to the point of becoming useless, yet I was stronger and leaner than ever in my life. And how could I have traveled through history to find my soul mate, only to lose her in the end?

I jumped when I heard the doorbell and quickly threw on some clothes, buttoning my shirt as I hurried down the stairs. My mother had went into town for groceries and I was alone in the house for a while.

When I opened the door, there was a blond guy in a dark uniform holding a package. Really blond, almost white hair. I could see a white delivery truck parked in the drive behind him.

"Don't I know you?" I asked him.

"I don't think so," he smiled, showing perfect white teeth as he handed me the package. "The past really has a way of catching up to you, doesn't it?" He was still smiling at me.

"What?" I said roughly.

"Sign here please." He held his clipboard out for me to sign.

"What was that you said, about the past?"

He took the clipboard from me and turned away, then stopped and looked back.

"Without our past, we wouldn't be who we are now."

"What are you talking about?" I yelled as he walked quickly away from me.

"There is no future without the past," he said mysteriously as he hurried back to his truck.

I shook my head and closed the door, my mind already returning to Kate. "What a kook," I said, and then I forgot all about him.

CHAPTER 36

I moped about the house for days, mourning the loss of Kate from the time I opened my eyes until the time I could fall into a restless sleep, filled with nightmares of Kate's lifeless body, the wind whipping the skirts of her pale blue dress as we floated off the cliff into the freezing water. The river took on a demon force in my dreams, the waves were arms pulling Kate away from me. I usually woke up sweating and unable to get back to sleep.

I was barely eating or sleeping and, after a few days, I told my mother I had to leave.

"I know son," she said quietly, sipping her morning coffee. "But first John, I want you to talk to me." She gave me a stern look, like she did when I was in high school. "I want to know who Kate is and why you're brooding around this house every day."

"I hope you have some time," I told her. "It's a long story."

"I have all the time in the world," she said, sipping her coffee.

"Okay, here goes," I said. "On November 6, 2010, I drove down Interstate Ninety from Seattle, then cut off onto Highway Eighty-Two and crossed the river into Oregon..."I talked for hours, telling her my story from the beginning til the point where I had opened my eyes in this world, omitting nothing. My voice broke when I told her of Kate's death and how I had leaped off the rock with her body.

She listened intently, only pausing to refill our coffee cups, until I had finished. When my story was done, she stood up without speaking, walked to the broom closet and came back with my crudely made moccasins in her hand.

I let out a groan as I stared at them. Talking about Kate for hours wasn't as painful as looking at those rough moccasins I had so clumsily sewn by the firelight, while I took care of Kate during her illness. "It wasn't a dream?"

"No son. I know that now. I don't know how, but it happened. I completely forgot about these until you mentioned it."

"I've gotta go," I said as I grabbed the moccasins from her.

"John." She took my arm before I could head out the door. "Just please promise me you'll stay off the bridges."

My throat closed up as I looked at her. Worry lines creased her forehead and her eyes looked scared. I hugged her tight, guilt gripping me as I thought about how I had worried her. "I *will* be back," I promised her.

I threw a change of clothes in a bag and went out to my car. My brothers had driven it here after I had been found. I headed east on Highway Eighty-Two, cut across through the Tri-Cities and followed Highway Twelve east toward the Walla Walla River. I drove slowly as the road paralleled the river, feeling closer to Kate the further east I went. My heart felt lighter as I looked at the river and the fog was finally beginning to clear from my brain.

When I saw a gun shop, I whipped the wheel and turned into the parking lot, emerging from the store after only a few minutes, a new survival knife strapped to my leg in a black nylon case. It didn't seem quite as good as the old Bowie, but I felt more like myself with it attached to my leg.

I continued on east and turned in at a small boat ramp on the river. I really thought of it as my river after all the time I had spent on it. It had been a means of survival for us and I knew I would never look at it the same way again.

I left my car in the lot beside a couple pickups with empty boat trailers behind them and started walking along the river, but nothing looked the same as it did before. There were more trees now, taller, older trees, there were fences that hadn't been there before and I could hear constant noises of traffic on the road and planes overhead. It looked the same, but not, and it was almost impossible to get my bearings.

I walked for miles, not sure where I was or where I was going, but the further I got from any civilization, the closer I felt to Kate. I sat down on a log as my mind wandered, Kate's face floating across my vision. I scratched the healing wound on my leg as I thought about how I had let go of her body. Why couldn't I have held on? I could have given her a decent burial here, with a nice marble head stone. Instead, I had let her body drift away to wash up who knows where. I had jumped, thinking I'd join her in the next life. Why was I still here without her? Dammit! I shook my head and sighed as I sat there, the warm spring sun beating on my back. I lay back in the new spring grass and stared up at a bright blue sky with a few cumulus clouds floating by. I swear, I could see her little round pixie face in each cloud that passed over me. I knew then, as I lay there in the warm sunshine, that this was how it would be the rest of my days. I was doomed to the present time, with no future in sight without her.

So I stayed out there, as far as possible from other people.

When I scared up a bunny, I grabbed that knife off my leg and, with a flick of my wrist, I put it into the rabbit hard enough that the point of the blade was sticking out the other side. I built a small fire and skinned the rabbit, then skewered it on a stick and held it over the fire, turning it constantly. I felt more at home than I had since I opened my eyes, if only I had Kate here to share it with me.

When it got dark, I curled up on the cold, wet ground by my fire and fell asleep. I still dreamed of Kate, but instead of horrible nightmares, I saw her dancing and twirling around the small cabin, her blue eyes sparkling in the firelight. I slept better than any time since I had awakened in this future time without her.

I stayed out there for days, it may have been a week; I kind of lost all track of time in my wanderings. I lived as I had in the past, from sunup until I fell asleep by my fire at night. I wandered the woods and river, lost and alone, caught between two worlds, unable to return to the one, unwilling to rejoin the other.

I dreamed of echoes one night, as I slept by my small fire with the cold seeping from the ground into my body. The dream was weird and made no sense, but I remembered it clearly the next morning. I was standing on a bluff overlooking the Columbia River and I heard Kate call my name. It echoed off the surrounding mountains, resonating over and over. On and on it echoed. Kate's musical lilting voice echoing my name again and again, each echo quieter than the one before.

I sat over my fire the next morning, without even a cup of hot coffee to warm me, and mulled over the dream. I could still hear the sound of my name echoing through my mind; Kate's musical, lilting tone sounding like sweet music in my head. The pain through my heart was excruciating, yet I held onto the sound of her voice throughout the day, as it reverberated through my mind. The single word, Kate calling my name, continued its echo as I walked and hunted.

I walked upriver for a couple days, then turned around and started back. I hadn't found where the cabin had been or anything that seemed familiar. I hunted as I walked, sometimes making a kill, other days going hungry, but never leaving the river. The pain and nightmares were duller out here, so I stayed, not knowing where I was going or what I would do with my life. I just knew that I felt closer to Kate out here and I didn't want to leave. She was in my thoughts constantly. I could picture her so clearly, walking along the river beside me as I hunted. As I sat by my fire each night, I almost felt as if she was there with me. I caught myself talking to her occasionally, as if she *were* there with me. I knew I was probably losing my mind, but I didn't care. Did I wish I had drowned in that river, instead of finding real love and then losing her? No. How does the saying go? It's better to have loved and lost, than never to have loved at all? It was worth the pain I was suffering now to have held her small hand even one time. To look once into those sparkly, ice-blue eyes and see the love and laughter shining out of them. No, the saying is true, I would never have tried to end it all, had I known how much I had to live for.

CHAPTER 37

I was sitting on a bit of a hill one day on the north side of the river. I wasn't sure, but it seemed like the most familiar place I'd been to. There was nothing I could point to and say, yes, this is where the cabin was, or this was my hunting grounds. It was just a feeling I had, as if I could feel Kate here, as if I could smell her in the fresh air. There were tall trees here, but I had a nice view of the river between their trunks. The sun dappled the ground as it shone through the trees and it felt warm on my back as I sat there. I had bathed in the cold water this morning, clothes and all, and I was sitting in the sun now, drying.

I could see Kate in my mind as I sat there, kneeling beside the river, doing laundry, looking up at me and laughing as I told her a stupid joke, her ice-blue eyes sparkling. I saw her sitting in front of the stone fireplace, placing her small hand in mine as I lifted her off the stone floor and twirled her around the cabin. I saw her dancing down the Oregon Trail, her arms out, saying how she wanted to fly like a bird. She always had the pale blue dress on when I saw her in my mind, it reached almost to the ground and made her waist look tiny. It was the one she was wearing when I met her and the one she was wearing as I jumped off the cliff with her body. I saw her moving through the trees down by the river, the pale blue dress dirty and ragged, but still beautiful to me. I thought about how many times I had stopped whatever I was doing, just to watch her. The way she moved, the way her long blond hair cascaded in waves down her back. I watched her turn away from the river and move slowly up the hill toward me, almost as if she were floating. My mind went back to the last time I'd seen her, with the dress floating around her as we fell toward the water. It hurt to see her constantly like this, every second of every day. I knew, no matter how long I lived, I would never get over her. I closed my eyes for a second, but when I opened them, her small form was still there, moving slowly up the hill. I shook my head to clear it, looked upriver, and then looked back. She still seemed to be almost floating toward me, the pale blue dress just touching the ground around her. I'd pictured her in my mind so many times, now I couldn't stop seeing her. Or was I going crazy like the old-time mountain men, staying out here so long I'd be talking to myself and seeing ghosts. I shook my head again and squinted my eyes, but yet I still saw her, she was almost in front of me now. I stood up as she reached me; I reached a hand out slowly and touched her face, unsure if she was really there. Was she real or was I delusional? Was it reincarnation? Was she a ghost?

"I knew you'd come here, John Baker."

I knew my mouth was hanging open in amazement, but I felt frozen, my hand still on her cheek. If she was a ghost, she sure felt and sounded real.

She was staring up at me with so much love and warmth in her beautiful blue eyes. I pulled her into my chest and held her tight. Tight enough to crush her delicate little bones. It was real, the same tiny, strong body, the same Kate smell. I could hear her crying into my chest, but I didn't loosen my hold. I was afraid if I did, I would wake up and she'd be gone. She finally pulled back and looked at my face. She had tears streaking her face and she smiled through them.

"Your face is all scruffy again and you look like you've hardly been eating."

I finally found my voice. "Kate," I croaked out, my voice rusty from lack of use. "How did you get here? I thought you were dead? No, you were dead, I know you were."

"I don't know, John. I woke up on the river bank with a pain in my back, just between my shoulders. When I made my way up the hill and saw the machines going by at a high rate of speed, I knew we had to be in two thousand and ten. When I couldn't find you, I knew you would come here, sooner or later." She paused, looking at the bewilderment on my face. Her eyes had the same ice-blue sparkle as always. "A man stopped beside the road and gave me a ride in his machine. It was so fast, the trees were a blur. I've been wandering along the river for days now, searching for you."

I turned her around and looked at her back. Her dress was torn and there was a scar where the tomahawk had been. "But you were dead." It didn't make any sense to me, but of course, what part of this crazy journey had made sense. I grabbed her and kissed her deeply. "I love you so much, Kate. God, I've missed you. I just can't believe you're really here. I thought I had lost you forever."

"I love you too, John Baker. I was afraid that I might never find you. I can only think that God brought me back to you."

"Yeah, well, it wouldn't be the first time. I'm never going to let you out of my sight again, I swear it." I picked her up into a bear hug, swinging her around and around. I could see the skirt of her blue dress floating as I twirled her. "Thank you, God," I said, when I had set her back on her feet. "Thank you for this miracle." I kept her hand in mine, afraid to let go of her for even a second.

"You hungry?" I asked finally, while I stared at her in amazement.

"I'm famished. I caught a fish two days ago, but I've had nothing since."

"Caught it how?"

Her blue eyes sparkled as she laughed. "With my bare hands...I swear it's true," she said at my astonished look.

"Let's go, little one," I put my arm around her shoulder and turned her around, back toward where I had left my car. "Let me introduce you to fast food in the future."

Author's Note

I crossed that old steel bridge from Oregon into Washington in July, 2013. As I looked down at the Columbia River, Dream of Echoes hit me like a freight train. Most of it anyway. I had been reading diaries of Pioneer Women and I've traveled most of the Oregon Trail. At least, what's accessible by road. I always thought it would be totally cool to travel back in time and just be a fly on the wall, experiencing history firsthand, without changing the future. I thoroughly enjoyed seeing it through John's eyes. Some of the events in the story are true. The Whitman Mission did exist, and the massacre did take place there. I hope you enjoyed John's journey as much as I did.

Karen C. Webb

Please leave a review at www.amazon.com or your favorite book retailer. Reviews help others to find an enjoyable story too. Thank you

Please enjoy this sneak peek of:

As Jericho Falls

I was in the middle of enjoying my fifteenth summer in my little corner of this beautiful, round blueberry we call earth. I was dreaming of escape, and even making plans for it, when life threw me a curveball. I had always been a dreamer; mama even called me a romantic, but never in a million years could I have dreamed up such as befell me that summer.

Our town of Jericho Falls, if you want to call it a town, sits up in the edge of the Blue Ridge Mountains, in Ashe County, North Carolina. We live—that is, my family and I—live on a farm about fifty miles from any real town. 'Fifty miles from nowhere, and one step closer to Hell,' mama used to say.

Jericho Falls is more of what you'd call a community, a small village of maybe ten houses in all, grouped around a small white church with a general store just down the dirt road, which also serves as the Post Office. It all sits along the banks of Jericho Creek, a pretty little creek with cold, clear water running down out of the mountains and filled with rainbow trout. A tall ridge runs along back of us; you can stand in this valley and see it's a gorge really, cut through these hills over millions of years by this swift-running mountain water.

Our farm, though, it sits further back up the gorge, maybe two miles up from Jericho Falls. Feels like a hundred miles if you're walking it. There's just our small, weathered house with a rusted tin roof, a falling down barn and about twenty acres of land. The barn was built into the side of a hill, and it actually leans a little as if it would fall over any day now.

My daddy, you see, is a horse trader and sometimes a moonshiner—'shiners—we call 'em here. When he quits drinking it long enough to sell it, that is. Sometimes him and a few of his horse trading buddies will sit out there, on the edge of the woods, and drink til late into the night. 'Shiners Convention,' daddy calls it.

Mama named me Lauren, on account of her and daddy went down to Lenoir one time back when they first met. They went to see one a them drive-in movies—Key Largo—it was called. It had Humphrey Bogart and Lauren Bacall in it, and mama said Ms. Bacall was the most beautiful, classiest lady she'd ever seen and if she ever had a daughter she was gonna name her Lauren.

Ain't none of us Martins ever been to school. What, you say? How is that possible in this day and age? This ain't a hundred years ago nor even fifty years ago, when Grandpa thought it was more important that daddy be helping on the farm instead a sitting on his butt in a classroom all day. Well, there's twenty-two miles of winding dirt road before we even hit the pavement to meet up with a school bus. And them dirt roads, I always hold my breath, whenever we do get to town. There's a hill on one side, because of the gorge, see, and the other side, well, Jericho creek sits off down in there, far below the road. The bank has gave way in spots. In the curves, you have to stay near the hill side or you're in danger of the bank falling out from under your vehicle, dropping you off down that cliff. There's even an old, rusted car down in there, lodged up against the tress, where somebody in the past fell off, then just left it there. I've had nightmares, ever since I was little, about falling off that dirt road.

'We take care of our own,' mama told me when I asked her about going to school. But I heard mama talking to daddy one time, when I was small, she said if the county people ever found out we'd never been in school, we'd all be in a heap a trouble. Well, she's home-schooled us up pretty good, me and my two brothers and my little sister Megan.

Well, it was two brothers, 'til some cantankerous ole mule daddy traded for went and kicked my little brother, Tommy. Kicked him right in his chest; stopped his heart, old Doc Roberts, down in Jericho Falls, told daddy. I can still see daddy, carrying Tommy's lifeless body in his arms, with tears running down his face. Only time I ever seen my daddy cry, at least, up until this crazy summer got over. Daddy had Tommy buried on the farm here, in our family plot, right alongside Grandma and Grandpa Martin.

Oh, you shoulda seen Tommy, that boy had somethin' special. 'A true gift from God,' mama always said. By the time he was seven years old, he was doing high school math, algebra and stuff that I struggle with now. And he was reading history books, boring books about the Civil War and the Roman Empire and he could quote you any passage from any book he read and even what page number it was on.

Daddy traded somebody for an old guitar and Tommy sat down with it, and within a few weeks, he'd taught hisself to play that guitar and, after a few more weeks, he was writing songs to go with his tunes. Mama has all them songs stored away now in her cedar chest. But I've seen her take 'em out occasionally, folded sheets of notebook paper held together with a rubber band. She cries as she reads them, but if she sees me watching, she pretends she's not. She always did need to be the strong one, strongest one of this whole family. Oh, maybe not physically, although I might lay odds on her there too, but mentally, she was the strong one. She was the glue that held us all together. Without her, we might of all been torn apart like the fluff of a dandelion and drifted away on the summer breeze.

My older brother, now—Will, his name is—he's the complete opposite of Tommy. 'Steadfast,' mama calls him. He loves nothing more than helping daddy on this two-bit farm and working with them half-broke horses and mules.

Not me, though, I got plans, plans and dreams. I dream of traveling the world, exploring all the places I'm always reading about. All of us Martin's reads a lot, on account of we ain't never had no TV, out here in the hills. After supper every day, each of us is likely to wander off to our bedrooms, picking up on whatever exciting adventure we was in the middle of. You could usually find me on a summer's afternoon, once the chores were done, laying back in the sweet green grass of daddy's pasture, sometimes surrounded by the sweet scent of wildflowers, reading books of faraway places and adventures. Usually don't take long though, if I'm still enough, 'til one of daddy's trade horses will be sniffing around me, blowing air on my head while it tries to figure out what I'm doing laying down in the middle of its lunch table. Sometimes they'll graze all around me; I listen to the sounds of the grass ripping in their teeth while I read.

But not today. Today, my little sister Meg is down with a fever and since daddy and Will are both working down at the sawmill—filling in while a couple guys are gone—then I guess it's on me to go for help.

"Go fetch Mrs. Parker," mama yelled out the door at me.

I come running from the garden where I'd been pulling weeds. Must be serious if she wants me to fetch that old witch, I thought. She's not a witch, really, even though she kinda looks like one. People like her, I've heard 'em called Mountain Sorcerers, but that ain't true neither. They're healers, is what they are. Mrs. Parker is a faith healer. Supposedly she says a passage from the bible while she holds the hand of the afflicted, but I read the Bible, cover to cover, on account a how we ain't got no TV, and I never did find no passage that said, 'read me and thou shalt be healed.'

But I seen it, though. I seen it with my own two eyes. We was in church one Sunday and Mrs. Parker was there, sitting in the pew just behind us. Jane Crockett brought her boy, Petey, over to Mrs. Parker and showed her his hands. That boy had warts all over both hands, big, nasty, ugly warts, that made me want to throw up, they was so ugly. Well, Mrs. Parker took those warty hands in hers, closed her eyes and commenced to whispering. I could see her lips moving, but for the life of me I couldn't make out a word she said. Then mama elbowed me in the ribs and I had to turn around and sit down.

Well, I didn't see Petey again for about a month, on account a how we ain't the most regular churchgoers and all. But, when I saw him again, his hands was as clean and wart free as yours or mine. Mrs. Parker talked them warts off, that's what mama said.

These mountains have lots of secrets—secrets they been holding for a thousand years. Secrets people outside of these hills don't usually get to know, and some that us in the hills don't know either, as I was about to find out.

So today, I gotta go and fetch Mrs. Parker back for Meg. Ordinarily, I could jump bareback on one of daddy's trade horses, but he'd sold the last one a few days ago. So I gotta hotfoot it near two miles, mostly uphill. I think they call it hotfooting around these parts cause in the summertime, most of us go barefoot. Most of us kids, anyhow. And that dirt road is doggone hot on the feet, unless they're tough as a ten-penny nail, like mine are.

But Megan, we gotta take care of her. She's my baby sister, the baby of the family. With her blond curls and big, blue eyes, I always thought she looked like a baby doll. I used to dress her up when she was smaller, pretending that she *was* one of my dolls. If mama was heartbroken over losing Tommy, losing Meg would just kill her, I'm sure of it.

My mind began to wander, as I strolled along the dirt road. I didn't notice the bright Mountain Laurel bushes as I walked, nor the bees that flitted from one bright pink blossom of it to the next. I didn't see the rich green of the Kudzu vines, snaking up the trees like it planned to choke the very life from them. I didn't hear the sound of Jericho Creek neither, as it trickled across stones and splashed its way down this mountain. No, I missed the world around me, cause I was busy with one of my daydreams. I pondered on what it would be like to live in one a them big, two-story houses in a subdivision, like I'd read about. To come home every day from my nice office, driving a shiny new car, and pulling it into a driveway made of concrete, instead of sand and mud. I saw myself clearly, in this fantasy of mine, opening the door to that big house, setting my briefcase down on a white tile floor, and kissing my handsome husband. Then making dinner for the two of us, in a kitchen that was all warm wood and granite countertops, with a big island in the middle, where my Prince Charming would sit down on a stool and talk to me while I chopped vegetables. Then I would pop a roast into an oven that was built into the wall, with a second oven just above it. I never did figure out what that second oven was there for. But I had read about it and even seen pictures in magazines, so it was there in my dream, just the same. I also had all kinda gizmos and gadgets in this fantasy of mine, computers and laptops, cellular telephones and epads or ipads, whatever they're called. It would take me years just to figure out how to work all this stuff, if my dreams ever did come true, that is.

I daydreamed my way right on up to Mrs. Parker's door, scattering chickens as I crossed the yard. Their house—Mrs. Parker and her husband, Bill—looked much the same as ours. Weathered, unpainted wood siding with a rusty tin roof and a porch across the front. I could hear the old boards creak as I crossed it and knocked on her door.

Mrs. Parker herself opened the door and smiled when she saw me. "Well, Lordy me, if it ain't young Lauren Martin. What brings you out here, child?"

"Mama sent me to fetch you back for my little sister Meg. She's powerful ill, down with a fever."

"Sure, sure. Well come on in, child. I was just making some lunch, have a bite with me before we make that long, sweaty walk."

"Yes, ma'am." I was pretty hungry, after all. Nothing like a long walk and some serious fantasizing to work up an appetite. I sat down at her kitchen table while Mrs. Parker dished up country ham and red-eye gravy, and fresh, homemade biscuits, all hot from the oven.

While we ate, Mrs. Parker asked me about Megan. "How longs she been sick?"

"More 'n a week, now. We thought she was getting some better, but this morning, she was just all burning up with the fever."

"How come you didn't go for Doc Roberts? Woulda been 'bout the same walking distance for ya."

"Doc Roberts is off on his summer fishing trip. Won't be back for two weeks."

"I see." Mrs. Parker stood up, cleaning up our few dishes. "Don't get up child," she said when I stood up to help. "I'll just clean up here and pen my chickens up, case I don't make it back afore dark."

She left me sitting there at her table, while she went to chasing chickens. I watched her out the window. Them chickens didn't want to go into their pen this early, but once the sun starts to set, try to keep 'em out. Chickens knows that there's some dangers lurking around these mountains in the dark.

I was starting to giggle, as I watched that old woman, chasing them chickens around and trying to shoo 'em toward their pen, when, of a sudden, I heard a noise, coming from upstairs. Which is strange, cause this house, just like ours, ain't got no upstairs.

There, I heard it again. I stared at the ceiling for a minute, listening to a tap, tap, tapping, an almost musical drumbeat of tapping. Then I looked back out the window at Mrs. Parker, wrangling them chickens. If she was outside, and Mr. Parker was at work, down at the mill, then where was that sound coming from? I stood up, still staring at the ceiling, and walked toward the living room. I found nothing in the living room and the sound seemed to be coming more from the back of the house, so I peeked in the door of a bedroom, which opened just off the living room, the way these old houses do. It was obviously Mr. and Mrs. Parker's bedroom, although it was neat as could be. A huge, four-poster bed set smack in the middle, made up all neat with a patchwork quilt. There was nothing else of interest, so I closed that door and stepped back into the living room. There was one more door, aside from a front door that led outside, but it was on a different wall. I opened this other door and found another bedroom, I assumed a spare bedroom; it was bare, just a bed in the middle, also made up neat as a pin, and an old bureau on one wall. I heard the tapping again—I looked up at the ceiling, there was a trapdoor, with a set of stairs leading up. Not stairs, exactly, but one of them folding ladders that pulls down from the ceiling. It was open now and there was that sound again, tap, tap, tapping, just above me. I looked behind me—still no sign of Mrs. Parker—then I started to climb. I know I shouldn't have—you just don't go into somebody's house and climb into their attic, uninvited. But like mama always said, curiosity killed the cat—so I climbed, the tapping growing louder with each step I took up that rickety ladder. As my head cleared the hatchway into the attic, what did I see? A boy, a pale teenage boy, tapping away at wooden poles with a wooden spoon, making a sort of music, I guess. He saw me; his eyes met mine and his music stopped while he stared. I don't remember climbing on up or crossing the attic to stand right in front of him, but I guess I did, cause suddenly, here I was, staring at a boy in a cage, with bars made of upright wooden poles, poles that stretched from floor to ceiling, and…he was naked as a Jaybird. Oh, he had pants, all right. He had his right arm out, like a waiter with a towel over it, holding a pair of black pants across his forearm.

Coming soon to all major print and ebook retailers.